Kittredge walked away but didn't go to the grocery store. Instead he went to the barber shop. In case there was any chance of coming into contact with the girl he wanted to look a little less begrimed and saddle-worn. He wondered what the relationship was between the girl and Sherman.

'That fella Sherman don't say a lot,' he reflected.

When he got up from the barber's chair he felt a whole lot better.

'Which way to the Rafter W?' he asked.

The barber did not immediately reply and Kittredge had to repeat the question.

'A few miles out of town,' the barber replied. 'Follow the trail north till you come to a cut-off. The Rafter W is signed further down.'

Kittredge thanked the barber and stepped to the door. It opened in his face and a couple of bewhiskered men brushed by him. Outside, their horses were tied to the hitchrack and he glanced at their brands: Spanish Bit. He returned to the Black Hat saloon where his horse was still tethered, climbed into the saddle and swung off down the main street. The town soon petered out in a jumble of old shacks and adobes. Glancing down, he could see lines in the dust left by carriage wheels.

That's probably Sherman and the girl, he thought.

He was still reflecting on what the relationship might be between them when something made him draw his horse to a halt. He listened carefully. After a few moments his ears detected the faint clatter of horses' hoofs. He looked around for cover. A little way ahead, situated just off the trail, was a clump of prickly pear mixed with mesquite with a small hill back of it. He rode into it and waited. A considerable time seemed to pass and he was beginning to wonder whether he had been wrong. Then a voice from behind him made him realize he had not been wrong but careless.

'Put your hands up. We got you covered.'

Whoever it was must have circled round. That meant they had been deliberately seeking him. From what he had heard of their horses, he reckoned there were at least two. No, probably just two. He remembered the two *hombres* who had pushed by him coming out of the barber shop. He needed to know where the other one was situated.

'Sure. Just take it easy.'

'Keep your mouth shut,' another voice called. 'And drop your gunbelt.'

Kittredge had a fair idea of where the two men were placed behind him. Maybe he was calculating this all wrong but that was a chance he had to take. As he slowly reached down for his gunbelt he dug his spurs into the buckskin's flanks. The horse jerked forward and Kittredge flung himself sideways and low as a rifle cracked and a bullet went flying over his head. Kittredge was leaning out at a sharp angle. As he held the reins in one hand he reached for his Colt with the other and fired back at the puff of smoke rising from the hillside. The man back there with the rifle had been a little slow in taking cover and Kittredge's bullet shattered his skull as though it was a pumpkin. Even for Kittredge it was a lucky shot. There was a succession of booms from the other man's rifle but the buckskin was galloping at pace and Kittredge knew he had nothing to worry about.

With some difficulty he hauled himself upright in the saddle and let the horse have its head before bringing it to a halt. He thought about going back and looking for the other man but decided against it. He remained still for a while, listening for any sounds of pursuit, but there was none. He reckoned the second bushwhacker had had enough. His action had taken them by surprise. The gunman was probably high-tailing it back to town. Kittredge had been negligent in allowing them the element of surprise but they had been more careless. They had given him an option and he had taken it.

Once he was satisfied that no one was on his back trail, Kittredge rode on. It was getting late in the afternoon and the sun was low. He was beginning to think he must have gone wrong somewhere when he arrived at the cut-off. As if to confirm that he was on the right track, the wagon seemed to have turned at this point. He left the main trail and kept riding. There were a few cattle on the range with their ears cut in a distinctive jingle bob. Presently he came to the signpost which carried the symbol for the Rafter W.

Seems pretty clear, Kittredge thought to himself.

For the first time he began to have doubts about the wisdom of coming out here. What did he know of Sherman or the Rafter W? Then he thought of the girl and carried on riding.

*

As Tad Sherman drove the wagon into the yard of the Rafter W, the door to the ranch house opened and the owner of the ranch appeared on the veranda. Sherman drew the wagon to a halt, dropped to the ground and walked round to assist his passenger alight. As she took his hand she gave him a quick glance.

'Thank you, Mr Sherman. I'm much obliged.'

Sherman nodded and touched the brim of his hat. The girl flounced up to the veranda and kissed her grandfather.

'You and Sherman were gone a long time,' he remarked. 'I was startin' to get worried.'

'There's really no need, and besides I'm sure Mr Sherman is more than capable of handling any little eventualities.'

'Maybe so.'

She moved past him into the house. Sherman was handing over the wagon to one of the ranch hands. When the girl had gone he turned to her grandfather.

'Mr Waggoner,' he said. 'Could I have a word?'

The ranch owner nodded. 'Sure. Come inside.'

When they were seated he handed his foreman a glass of whiskey.

'So. You wanted to say something to me?' he asked.

'Yeah. While Miss Trashy was doin' her shoppin', I looked in at the Black Hat saloon. Some of Gonsalez's boys were there, lookin' for trouble. They found it.'

'Really, Sherman,' Waggoner replied. 'I'm not sure I can rely on you to keep my granddaughter safe if you will persist in getting into these little contretemps.'

Sherman's face was blank.

'Not me,' he said. 'Another fella. There was a bit of gunplay. I tell you, I think we've found our man.'

'In what sense?'

'I've never seen anyone so quick with a gun. And he don't drink. He was in there askin' for sarsaparilla.'

'Mm. That's always a good sign. A man may be useful with a gun, but once he starts on the liquor he's liable to lose it.'

'That's what I thought. Anyway, I told him to ride on out to the Rafter W. Thought you might like to take a look.'

Waggoner took a sip of the whiskey. 'Good thinkin',' he said. 'I could always use an extra hand or two around the place. Particularly if what you say is correct.'

Sherman finished his drink. 'Guess I'll get on over to the bunkhouse,' he said.

He got to his feet. On his way out he looked for a glimpse of Miss Trashy but she had gone to her room. He made his way to the bunkhouse, stopping to look at himself in the cracked mirror hanging above a water trough outside. His face was lined and leathery. There were deep wrinkles around the corners of his eyes. Maybe he was just too old for Miss Trashy. She was a beautiful, spirited young woman. What did he expect her to see in him? He couldn't blame her lack of interest. Maybe the time had come for him to move on.

He went inside the building, threw himself across his bunk, pulled out a pouch of tobacco and some papers and rolled himself a smoke. The bunkhouse was deserted and after a time he got up and moved across to the corrals, where the horses for the remuda were gathered. Their smell was strong in his nostrils. He was walking back towards the bunkhouse when he heard the sound of hoofs. A few moments later Kittredge rode into the yard.

'Howdy,' Sherman said.

Kittredge climbed from the leather.

'You found the place OK?' Sherman asked.

'Yeah.'

'I'll roust up one of the boys to take care of the horse. Grab your things and come with me.'

Kittredge took his rifle and blanket together with a few other things and they walked over to the bunkhouse. Sherman indicated a spare bunk.

'Make yourself at home.'

Kittredge took a look around.

'Seems kinda quiet,' he said.

'Most of the boys are out on the range. They'll be headed back soon. In the meantime, the boss would like to have a word with you.'

Kittredge raised an enquiring eyebrow.

'Seb Waggoner. He's the owner. I'll take you over. How about some coffee first?'

Sherman made the coffee while Kittredge spread out his things.

'Sure appreciate this,' he said.

'Appreciate what?'

'Givin' me someplace to stay. I wasn't intendin' to remain in Arrowhead but it's nice to have a mattress under my back.'

'Been ridin' long?'

'A whiles.' He was about to mention the trail drive

but then decided against it.

'Lookin' for a job?'

Kittredge was thinking of the girl. 'I would have booked in at the hotel if I'd had the dollars,' he said.

Sherman poured out the thick black mixture. 'Well, I can't say but Mr Waggoner might be lookin' to take on an extra hand.'

Kittredge nodded. 'What's your role?' he asked. You ramroddin' the outfit?'

'Me? I been with the Rafter W for a long time. Worked my way up to bein' top screw.'

'I guess you know most of the brands around here?'

'Yup. Why do you ask?'

Kittredge swallowed a mouthful of the black coffee. 'A couple of varmints tried bushwackin' me. If they're who I think they are, their horses were carryin' a Spanish Bit brand.'

Sherman eyed him closely. 'You don't miss much,' he commented.

Kittredge did not reply.

'The Spanish Bit is a long ways from here, down near the border. Most ranchers round these parts know about it. The ranch is a front for the Comancheros. Most of their stock comes from cattle rustlin' and tradin' with the Comanche. I figure there's Rafter W stock amongst them.'

'Why doesn't somebody do somethin' about it?' asked Kittredge.

'They're clever. It's hard to pin anything on 'em. But there's more to it than that. They run the whole country down there near the border. The Spanish Bit is just a part of it. The entire territory is outside the law.'

'I've been wonderin' why those bushwhackers jumped me. I figure they must have been connected with the varmints we mixed it with in the saloon.'

'Sure, you're right. Leastways, that's how I would see it.'

'Then the Comancheros are operatin' as far north as the area around Arrowhead?'

'Like I said, it don't take you long to catch on.'

Kittredge finished his coffee. 'Is that why you're talkin' about Waggoner offerin' me a job?' he said. 'I ain't been here but five minutes and I can see there seems to be a shortage of hands for a ranch this size.'

'Maybe I've said too much. I'll take you over to the ranch house and let Waggoner do the talkin'.'

Kittredge raised himself from the bed. 'One other thing,' he said.

'Yeah? What's that?'

'Who was the young lady I saw you with in town?'

Sherman shot Kittredge a sudden sharp look.

'Is she some relation of Waggoner?'

Sherman's eyes held those of Kittredge for a moment longer. 'She's his granddaughter,' he replied. 'She's called Patricia but folks call her Trashy.' What might have been the beginnings of a smile lifted a corner of Sherman's mouth.

'You know,' he added, 'it's goin' to be interestin' havin' you along.'

'I haven't spoken to Waggoner yet,' Kittredge replied. 'What makes you think I'm gonna accept even if he does offer me a job?'

16

The suggestion of a grin remained on Sherman's face. 'Because you ain't gonna just forget what those Comancheros tried to do to you. I'd say you almost got a personal stake in what happens round here now.'

'Those Comancheros ain't likely to forget what we did to them either,' Kittredge remarked.

Sherman moved towards the door. 'Better see Mr Waggoner,' he said.

During the days that followed Kittredge spent a long time in the saddle. He had no illusions about Waggoner's real reason for hiring him. Whatever uses Kittredge might have around the ranch, he was being hired mainly for his gun. Kittredge had no qualms about that. As Sherman had implied, he had a personal interest, since those gunnies had bushwhacked him. And that was something quite apart from Miss Trashy. He had watched out for that young lady the first day he spent at the ranch but he had not seen her. He decided that it might be a good idea to familiarize himself with the Rafter W range and what lay beyond.

It seemed a fine spread with plenty of grass and water. Out to the north and east there were other ranches – notably the Scissors – while to the west the land rose gradually towards a range of low hills. Riding south it was a different story. The rich pastures gradually gave way to long stretches of bunch-grass country before the desert began to make its presence felt. Kittredge didn't ride any further but he knew that the country beyond became wild and raw. He had ridden there before. Eroded by sun and wind, the land was

17

jagged and broken with only odd patches of green indicating the presence of an oasis. Tall spires and
battlements of red rock raised their impregnable
heights to the burning sky and canyons cut into the
tablelands like gashes across the face of the earth. An
army of men could hide up in that untamed wilderness,
which was one reason why the Comancheros roamed
unchecked.

Kittredge drew rein and built a cigarette. The sun
was burning in the sky and he knew how it would be
once he really got into the badlands. Sweat trickled
down his back and he took off his bandanna to wipe his
brow. He smoked till the cigarette was half-finished,
then drew his binoculars from his saddle-bags. Slowly
he let his eyes sweep the landscape, trying to fix it in his
mind because he knew it might be important to know it
later. A buzzard flew overhead, casting a shadow.

He had almost completed his examination of the
terrain when he spotted movement and a plume of
dust. He trained the glasses on the area for just a few
moments before lowering them, aware of the danger of
reflections. Those few moments were enough for him
to identify a wagon, which was being pulled by a couple
of mules. It had disappeared from sight but after a time
he picked out the dingy whiteness of its canvas against
the dull red background as it emerged from the concealment of a cluster of rocks.

'What the hell,' Kittredge muttered to himself.

He touched his spurs to the buckskin's flanks, being
careful not to reveal himself, and rode in the direction
of the wagon. He took shelter behind some bushes a

short distance away from the trail where he figured the wagon would pass by, and settled down to wait.

Presently he heard the rumble of wheels and, accompanied by a high-pitched whistle, the wagon came into sight. Kittredge could now get a proper look at it. The wagon was dusty and dilapidated and the canvas was torn in places. Scrawled across it in faded letters were the words: *Doc Grattan's Travelling Medicine Show and Mobile Trading Emporium*. The wagon was pulled by four tired looking mules and high on the driving seat sat a thin and lank man of middle years with a white goatee gathered to a twisted point. Despite the heat he wore a long black coat and on his head a tall stovepipe hat, from which long strands of white hair fell to his shoulders. He seemed to Kittredge like an apparition. The man was whistling tunelessly a melody which Kittredge eventually recognized as a song which had been popular in the Civil War: 'Eatin' Goober Peas', which, after a break, became 'Sweet Lorena'.

Kittredge watched in some amazement as the wagon came closer, then he became aware that he was faced with a slight difficulty. How was he to reveal himself to the newcomer without startling him unnecessarily? The matter was taken out of his hands when his horse, taking fright at the scent of the mules, suddenly decided to neigh, sidestepping and shaking its head at the same time. When Kittredge looked up the wagon had stopped and the strange driver was standing on the front board with a .50-calibre Sharps rifle pointed at his chest.

'Ride on out, friend!'

The man's voice was strangely deep and melodious and he spoke with a Georgia accent. Kittredge rode clear of the bushes.

'A body don't naturally hide unless he means mischief,' the man said.

'If I'd meant mischief you wouldn't have got this far,' Kittredge replied. 'I been watchin' you a long time.'

'Makes me wonder why you ain't got anythin' better to do.'

Kittredge decided that the best thing was to be entirely straight with the man.

'I ride for an outfit called the Rafter W,' he said. 'Just scoutin' the territory.'

The man's arm relaxed a trifle. 'The Rafter W? Would that be Seb Waggoner's spread?'

Kittredge tried not to show his surprise at the driver's mention of Waggoner.

'You know it?' he said.

The man's eyes had strayed to Kittredge's horse, checking the brand.

'Sure, I know it. How's that granddaughter of his?'

It seemed to Kittredge there was a gleam of amusement in the man's eyes. 'Ain't got to meet her yet,' he said. 'But Sherman's doin' fine.'

The man's arms sank lower and he let the rifle dangle from his hand.

'Sherman's a good man,' he said. At last he put the rifle down and held out his hand. 'Name's Grattan,' he said. 'Cass Grattan.'

'Dean Kittredge.'

'You headed back for the Rafter W?'

'Sure. I think I seen everything now.'

Grattan smiled. 'Includin' me. I'm surprised you ain't come across me before.'

'Like I say, I'm new. What about you? Where are you bound?'

'For Arrowhead eventually. Might take me a time to get there.'

Kittredge looked over the wagon. 'What's your line of business?'

'Just what it says. Medicine, horse-doctorin', cure-alls, general tradin'. Come, take a look inside the wagon.'

He climbed somewhat laboriously down from his perch and when he moved Kittredge observed that he favoured one leg.

'Leg wound,' Grattan said. 'Manassas. Kinda put me out of the war from the start. Leastways as a combatant.'

Kittredge slid from the saddle and followed him to the back of the wagon. Taking hold of the drawstring, Grattan opened the flap. Kittredge hadn't known what to expect but the scene inside took him by surprise. The interior held a jumble of objects, some of which he would have been at a loss to explain. There were pelts and furs, blankets, mirrors, beads, items of clothing, feathered head-dresses, wood and stone carvings, anti-quated trade guns – rifled caplocks and flintlocks – pots and pans and other utensils, and a litter of small items which might have been toys. Above all there were bottles stacked in boxes and crates and lined up on shelves; Kittredge could not see how they didn't just fall to the floor and smash. Hanging from hooks attached

21

to the canvas wagon cover were some gaudy costumes.

'Oh yeah,' Grattan said. 'You can add actin' to that little list I gave you.'

He looked Kittredge up and down. 'I don't suppose you've ever trod the boards? A fine figure of a man like you would make an acceptable Greek hero or a passable Romeo. How are you with the classics?'

'Can't say I know 'em too well,' Kittredge replied.

'Well, if you're ever in Arrowhead or any of the other towns in this god-forsaken corner of our otherwise fair land, look me up. There could be a whole new career just waitin' for you.'

'I'll bear it in mind,' Kittredge said.

Together, he and Grattan returned to the front of the wagon and Grattan, with some difficulty, climbed back on to his seat. Kittredge stepped into leather. Before riding away he turned back to Grattan.

'Seems to me like you can't be doin' a lot of trade where you're comin' from.'

Grattan gave a crooked smile. 'That's just where you're wrong,' he said. 'Besides, I can find business anywhere. It's just what you're used to. Figure I could strike a deal with a rattlesnake if I put my mind to it.'

Kittredge laughed. 'That include the Comancheros?' He didn't expect an answer. 'Take care, old-timer,' he said.

Although the man probably wasn't that old, Kittredge was somehow thinking of him that way. Grattan smiled a gap-toothed smile and spat into the dust.

'Since you mention the Comancheros,' he said, 'and

because I wouldn't like to see a young fella like you get into anything he'd do better to avoid, I'll give you a bit of advice. Watch out for an *hombre* goes by the name of El Serpiente.'

'Funny sort of name,' Kittredge commented.

Grattan paused. 'So long, young'un,' he said. 'I'll look out for you. Give my regards to Sherman and old Waggoner.'

He leaned out and spat again. 'Oh yes,' he added. 'And Miss Trashy too.'

He jerked on the reins and the mules took the strain. Kittredge watched till the wagon was hidden by a cloud of dust, then he set his spurs to the buckskin's flanks and began the ride back to the Rafter W.

It was late when he arrived and there were no lights inside the bunkhouse. He was just finishing feeding and currying the horse when there was a noise outside and the stable door opened. Instinctively Kittredge spun round, his gun in his hand, before he recognized the figure of Sherman.

'Sorry,' he said, 'I guess it just comes natural. Kinda forgot where I was.'

He dropped the gun back into its holster.

'That's OK,' Sherman said. 'Just as long as you take the time to make sure you know who it is before you start shootin'.'

'You're up late,' Kittredge said.

'Couldn't sleep. I heard you ride in. How far did you get?'

'Pretty far. Just about where the country starts gettin' really rough.'

'See anythin'?'

'If you mean Comancheros, nope. But I did run into somebody. He sends his regards, by the way.'

In the gloom, Sherman's face looked puzzled, then he smiled.

'Don't tell me,' he said. 'Doc Grattan and his crazy wagon.'

'Yeah. Right first time. He sure seems a strange old buzzard.'

'You're right. Remind me to tell you about him sometime. But just now I got some news for you. You'd better get some sleep because you got an early start in the mornin'.'

Kittredge slung his saddle up on the rack.

'Yeah? What you got in mind?'

'Not me. Mr Waggoner. Seems his daughter wants to pay another visit to Arrowhead and you're the man to accompany her there.'

Kittredge remained calm. 'Sure, if that's what Mr Waggoner and Miss Trashy want. But why me?'

Sherman shrugged his shoulders.

'Just make sure you bring her back safe.'

'What, should I expect trouble?'

'Nope, but you've seen how things stand around here. If it was down to me, I reckon I'd keep Miss Trashy right here on the ranch, but she likes to have her own way and her grandfather lets her have it.' He turned to go.

'Oh, and one other thing. You might be the one ridin' shotgun on Miss Trashy, but you can be sure Waggoner will have his boys on the watch for her. You

24

might not see anythin' of 'em, but they'll be around somewheres.'

The door opened and closed and Sherman was gone. Kittredge waited for a while before making his way out of the barn. Outside it was a clear, balmy night with a sky full of stars. A gentle breeze had arisen and he felt its cool breath on his cheeks. He stopped to look up at the sky and breathed deeply. Then he went inside the darkened bunkhouse.

CHAPTER TWO

High above the scarred landscape, the man known as El Serpiente sat on a ledge watching the scene beneath. Behind him the stone houses of the pueblo merged into the shadows of a huge cavern fringed with cedars. Sunlight glinted on the waters of a stream flowing through the box canyon 1,000 feet below. The place was well chosen as a hideout. There was a rough, difficult path up the side of the mesa from the canyon floor, but it was well hidden and easily defended. The mesa itself was a maze of canyons and deep grassy valleys, the ideal place to hide and keep stolen cattle. The whole place was remote and impregnable.

Right now, looking through his binoculars, El Serpiente could see a group of his men driving another small herd of cattle towards the mesa. Satisfied that negotiations with the Comanche must have gone well, he laid the binoculars aside and glanced up at the sound of footsteps. Coming towards him was the lithe figure of his woman Carmelita, carrying some washing. As she approached he grabbed her by the waist and the washing dropped to the floor. She made to pick it up but he pulled her close to him, kissing her hard on the lips. His fingers strayed across her tight blouse. For a few moments his hands closed on her taut breasts, then she succeeded in pushing him aside.

'You carry on drinking,' she said. 'I have things to do and then I make myself ready.'

Gonsalez grinned. 'You do that,' he said.

Quickly she walked away, not bothering to collect the washing. Gonsalez watched her with lust in his eyes as she entered an ancient grey, two-storey house and then vanished from his sight. Once inside she breathed deeply as she readjusted her garments. She wiped her hand across her mouth as if to remove the taste and smell of Gonsalez's liquor-tainted breath. She had succeeded in escaping him but it was only for a short period of time. Soon he would be finished drinking and then. . . . She didn't like to think about it.

It hadn't always been this way but it seemed a long time ago since things were any different. Gonsalez had changed. She knew he had other women, but she didn't know whether he treated them as badly. He had changed so much that she no longer recognized him. He had become corrupted by all the killing and thieving. The living had been good once but it was no longer enough for Gonsalez, even though he was now the boss of his own outfit and the reputation of El Serpiente was growing, from the Rio Grande to the Sangre de Christo mountains.

The only obstacle now to his ambition, as far as Gonsalez was concerned, was the man who had

27

financed his operations, Jensen Crudace, the owner of the Spanish Bit. Crudace had been a useful ally but now Gonsalez saw him as an obstacle. One way and another, things were coming to a head.

Kittredge was kept waiting by Miss Trashy. He had been expecting to drive the buckboard, like Sherman, but it seemed Miss Trashy wanted to drive herself and was taking the one-seater buggy. When she eventually appeared he felt it was well worth the wait. She had done her auburn hair up, revealing the lines of her neck. She wore a long blue dress with white gloves and the effect was to make her appear more mature, more sophisticated. For a moment she stood looking down on Kittredge from the veranda and he could only admire how lovely she looked. Just in time he recalled himself and, taking her outstretched hand, he helped her down the steps and into the buggy. He climbed into leather, then she snapped her whip. The buggy moved forward and he rode slightly behind in order that the dust of his horse would not disturb her. As they passed out of the yard he turned his head to see Sherman watching from the bunkhouse door. He nodded but there was no response. For a few moments Kittredge felt rather silly but when they had passed out of the immediate vicinity of the ranch house he began to feel better.

It was a sunny morning. Little white cloudlets drifted through the azure. Ketteridge was congratulating himself on his good fortune. To be this close to the lady who had drawn his attention that afternoon in

28

Arrowhead seemed almost too good to be true. The sunlight fell on her hair and sprinkled highlights among its auburn tresses. She was not wearing a bonnet. From what he could tell, she seemed to be very competent at driving the buggy.

They went along at a crisp pace and it wasn't long before they had turned on to the main trail into Arrowhead and were passing the spot where Kittredge had been bushwhacked. Almost by force of habit his eyes skimmed the terrain but it was a peaceful scene with no signs of anything untoward. The outlying houses of Arrowhead hove into view and before long they were turning into Main Street. So far they had not exchanged any words.

Kittredge was expecting her to halt outside the general store or the clothing emporium, but instead she carried on past them before pulling the buggy to a halt outside an establishment bearing the words: *Ma Kennedy's Eating House.* Uncertain of how to proceed, Kittredge dismounted, quickly tied his horse to the hitchrack, then approached the buggy. Miss Trashy held out her hand and he helped her step down.

'Mr Kittredge,' she said, 'I understand you are not a drinking man. Perhaps you would care to join me for morning coffee?'

Kittredge wasn't sure whether she was being ironical, whether she might be making fun of him. Perhaps there was even an element of criticism in her words. She seemed to be talking straight.

'I'd be right honoured,' he said.

She gave him the hint of a smile. He wondered what

he should do next, but she relieved him of further spec-
ulation by turning on her heel, mounting the steps to
the boardwalk, and entering the café. Inside it was cosy
and welcoming. The tables were neat with blue-checked
tablecloths and flowers in little vases. The place was
empty and Miss Trashy made her way to a corner table
by the window. Kittredge pulled out her chair and she
sat down while he hesitated before sitting down opposite her. Sunlight coming through the window
illumined her face and Kittredge noticed for the first
time a delicate sprinkling of freckles above her nose. It
touched him. Miss Trashy was at once both a lovely
woman and a girl. In their current context, she was con-
siderably more poised than he.

'Here comes Mrs Kennedy,' she said. 'Would you like
something to eat?'

A door at the back of the room had opened and a
large woman with white hair was approaching their
table.

'Good morning, Miss Waggonner,' she said.

Her glance strayed to Kittredge and then back to
Miss Trashy. 'I have some real nice doughnuts today,'
she said.

'Doughnuts will be fine,' Miss Trashy replied. 'And
some of your best coffee, of course.'

Mrs Kennedy departed but soon returned with a tray
of doughnuts and a pot of coffee. She reached down
two china cups and saucers from a dresser, then
returned to the kitchen, leaving the door just a little
ajar.

'You can pour,' Trashy said.

Kittredge concentrated on not spilling the coffee into the saucer.

'Milk?' he asked.

'Yes, but not too much.'

Kittredge took his coffee black. They each took a doughnut and Kittredge was relieved to see the gusto with which she bit into hers. As Mrs Kennedy had said, they were very good.

When Trashy had eaten half of her doughnut and taken a couple of sips of coffee, she looked at him.

'Mr Kittredge,' she said, 'are you a gunfighter?'

The question took him by surprise.

'I see you wear two guns. That's not usual.'

Kittredge recovered some of his equanimity.

'Is your father in the habit of employing gunmen?' he replied.

She emitted a tiny laugh like a tinkling bell. 'No, not so far as I'm aware,' she replied.

'Then I'm not a gunman.'

She looked away. Kittredge's gaze moved past her to the street where a buckboard was driving past the window. There were faint sounds coming from outside and somewhere further off a dog barked. All very natural, but it seemed far away.

'I'm sorry,' she continued. 'You must think me rather odd. It's just that there have been one or two incidents and I'm sure that my grandfather is worried. When Sherman brought me to town last time, I sensed that something had happened. And then you came.'

Kittredge let that comment ride. Instead he steered the conversation in a different direction.

31

'What sort of incidents?'

'Strangers passing through, cattle disappearing. I don't know. Nobody tells me anything. Grandfather thinks I'm still a child. He won't allow me to come into town on my own. That's another reason I sense that things are not right. It didn't use to be that way.'

Kittredge was feeling a growing confidence. 'You're free to be drinking coffee with me,' he said.

His glance rested on her for a moment and he thought he detected a faint flush on her throat and cheeks.

'Look out the window,' she replied.

Kittredge leaned forward. 'What am I lookin' for?' he said.

'Do you see a man outside the Black Hat? Wearing a blue shirt and a waistcoat?'

Kittredge saw him. He was partly concealed behind a stanchion.

'Who is he?' he asked.

'That will be Brigstock,' she said. 'One of my grandfather's top hired hands. So you see, we're not alone.'

Kittredge recalled Sherman's words about being watched. Was Waggoner's concern just a grandfather's normal solicitude, or was there more to it?

'I have shopping to do,' Trashy suddenly remarked.

She stood up and Kittredge followed suit. He made to move her chair but she was already past him and moving towards the door.

'Meet me in an hour,' she said.

Kittredge was taken aback by the suddenness of her departure. As the door closed behind her he stepped to

32

the counter. It was plain that he was expected to pay and he was thankful that he had his wallet with him. Ma Kennedy had already emerged. As he handed over the money she fixed him with a smile.

'Mr Sherman not coming into town today?' she asked.

'Nope.'

'Give him my regards when you see him.'

Kittredge stepped outside. The buggy was standing close by and he considered moving it. Instead he began to walk slowly down the street. He had started to familiarize himself with the country. Maybe it would be a good idea to get a sense of the lay-out of the town. It didn't take long. Arrowhead was like a hundred other towns he had passed through. Along the length of Main Street the weather-worn clapboard buildings faced one another, the same false-fronted structures: the general store, the saloon, the bakery, the eating house, the hardware store, the gunsmith's, the feed-and-hay store, the barber shop. On one corner stood the marshal's office opposite the bank.

He turned down at the intersection and came out on a back street where the livery stables and the blacksmith's workshop were situated. He walked to the far end of the street where there was a schoolhouse, then made his way back to Main Street, a little way along which stood an imposing building made of adobe. A sign along the front read *Jensen Crudace: Land and Cattle Company.*

Kittredge paused, thinking hard. *Jensen Crudace.* The name rang a bell but he couldn't think where he had come across it before. Maybe there was another name he was confusing it with. After a few moments he gave up the struggle and began to make his way back to the café to wait for Miss Trashy. On the way he looked for the figure of Brigstock outside the Black Hat saloon, but he wasn't there. Only then did he realize he had made a big mistake in letting Trashy out of his sight. Hell, he was supposed to be looking after her. She had left in such a rush that she had taken him unawares. He had been lulled into a false sense of security by the bland, peaceful appearance of the town. Now suddenly he was stung into action.

Quickly he made his way to the clothing emporium, but she wasn't there. He moved on to the general store but they had not seen her. He tried other places without success. The town wasn't so big that she could disappear for very long. Moving swiftly, he retraced his footsteps as far as the schoolhouse, although he knew there was little chance of her straying far from the main drag. When he rounded the corner by Crudace's Land and Cattle Company he breathed a sigh of relief. Along the street ahead of him he could see the unmistakable figure of Miss Waggoner walking back towards the buggy. She was in the company of someone else whom he recognized after a moment as Brigstock. He began to run and reached the vehicle at just about the same time as they did.

'You seem to be in something of a rush, Mr Kittredge,' she said.

He didn't know what to reply.

'It's all right,' she continued. 'It's been not much

34

more than an hour and in any case, Mr Brigstock here was on hand to help me.'

Kittredge and Brigstock exchanged glances. Kittredge didn't know what to make of the situation and he suspected that Brigstock felt the same.

'Perhaps, Mr Brigstock, you can help me into the buggy,' Miss Trashy continued.

Brigstock offered his arm and she climbed up to the driver's seat. Kittredge felt the slight.

'Thank you, Mr Brigstock,' she said. She turned to Kittredge. 'Mr Brigstock will accompany me.'

Without further ado she raised her whip and the buggy moved off. Brigstock went to get his horse and the pair of them met up at the end of the street, continuing together in the direction of the Rafter W.

The feeling of relief Kittredge had experienced at seeing Miss Trashy safe was superseded now by a variety of feelings, not least of which was confusion over her attitude towards him. She seemed to have changed so suddenly that he wondered what he might have done to upset her. He climbed into the saddle and moved off, still puzzling over the way things had gone. He thought back to his conversation with Miss Trashy and especially to her question as to whether he was a gunman. Did she perceive something about him of which he was unaware? Apart from any feelings he might have about Miss Trashy, he had taken on the Rafter W job because he had felt that there was common cause between him and Waggoner against the Comancheros. He had an issue with the Comancheros, but should he not deal with them on his own terms? He still felt guilty about leaving Miss Trashy unprotected. Mulling these things over, he came to the signboard indicating the boundary of the Rafter W. He looked out over the range, having a sudden sensation that he was being watched. He concluded that it was probably true, and rode on.

If Kittredge had come past Jensen Crudace's Land Company office a little later, he might have been surprised to see a somewhat unlikely individual being given admittance. Then again, he probably wouldn't have noticed anything because the man had hitched his horse a considerable distance away and was very careful that nobody noticed him. He was a tall man, lean as a rail, and he bore the dust of the trail with him. Jensen Crudace regarded him distastefully before ushering him to a chair. He took a cigar from a case on his desk but very pointedly did not offer one to his visitor. When he had lit up and inhaled he turned to him.

'You can tell Gonsalez from me that I'm not happy with his behaviour. I know what he's been doin' with the cattle.'

'I don't know what you mean. We take cattle, we barter cattle from the Comanche. We take the cattle to your hacienda, the Spanish Bit. You pay us. That is the arrangement.'

'Yeah, that's the arrangement. Trouble is too many of those beefs are goin' to Gonsalez. I don't know exactly what sort of a set-up he's got down there, but he's over-steppin' the mark.'

The man's face was like stone. 'I don't know what you mean. I come because you sent word you want to talk about something. I am only a go-between. I know nothing about El Serpiente.'

Crudace grinned. 'El Serpiente,' he sneered. 'Why do you call him that?'

'I didn't name him. Who knows? Perhaps because he is quick and poisonous like a snake. Maybe one day you will find out.'

'Is that a threat?'

'It is no threat. You ask me why he is known as El Serpiente. It is a guess.'

Crudace placed the cigar on the edge of an ashtray. 'Never mind all that,' he said. 'That has nothing to do with why I sent for you. The fact of the matter is, I want Gonsalez's assistance in a little matter here in Arrowhead.'

'You mean the Rafter W? It is a long way from the Spanish Bit.'

'Let's say I'm thinking of expanding. The country is nice around here. The Spanish Bit is one thing; this is something else altogether.'

'You also have the Scissors.'

'Exactly. I own the Scissors but it is too small. Now if the Rafter W should come up for sale at a knock-down price, well. . . .' He paused to allow his words to sink in.

'So you are thinking that a little more pressure from El Serpiente might help the owner to come to an agreement?'

'You are very astute, my friend.'

Crudace stood up. 'You can take a message to Gonsalez. Tell him I want some action. What Gonsalez has been doin' up till now has just been tinkerin' at the edges. Now I want some real pressure put on Waggoner, the owner of the Rafter W.'

'And what would be in it for El Serpiente?'

Crudace laughed. 'Some place for him to keep his cattle. Look, if I can get my hands on the Rafter W I wouldn't be too interested in the Spanish Bit. El Serpiente could have it. At a reasonable price of course.'

'And what is to stop El Serpiente taking the Spanish Bit for himself?'

'Because he knows my men have control there. Because he knows better than to try and get clever with me. El Serpiente might be able to put one over on a pack of sweatbacks and no-hope owlhoots, but he isn't stupid. He knows where his best interests are.'

The visitor got to his feet and walked to the door.

'Take care nobody sees you leave,' Crudace said.

The door closed and he took up his cigar. 'I will have to keep an eye on El Serpiente,' he reflected.

The arrangement with the Comancheros had stood him well so far. The Comancheros could be the ones to help get him the property he wanted, the Rafter W. But when the ranch was safely in his hands, it might be as well to deal with Mr Gonsalez.

There were no repercussions from Waggoner on the matter of having left Miss Trashy to her own devices when Kittredge got back to the Rafter W. In fact it was that young lady herself who thanked him for taking the time to accompany her. Again she had confounded him. He had been expecting her to adopt quite the opposite attitude, but she seemed to go out of her way to welcome him, meeting him as he rode into the yard. She smiled sweetly.

'I may be calling on your services again soon,' she said. 'That is, if Grandfather can spare you.'

Kittredge put his horse in the stable and went into the bunkhouse where a few of the boys were playing checkers. They looked up at him and he thought he read a certain degree of envy in their eyes. Evidently Miss Trashy had her admirers. Later, when he had eaten, Kittredge took a walk over to the corrals and found Sherman just coming out of the stables.

'How did it go with Miss Waggoner?' he said.

'Fine, but I don't think it's somethin' I want to do too often.'

'Yeah?'

'Not really my style, ridin' shotgun on a female.'

It was true. He had been grateful for the opportunity but at the same time it had felt awkward.

'Know what you mean,' Sherman replied.

Kittredge pulled out his tobacco pouch and cigarette papers. He rolled a thin, tight smoke and Sherman did the same. They lit up and leaned together on the corral rail.

'Some cattle gone missin' again,' Sherman remarked.

'Rustlers? Where do they go?'

'I got my suspicions. Can't prove anythin'.'

'That oldster Grattan mentioned some place called the Spanish Bit, said it was a front for the Comancheros. But it seems to be a good ways off.'

'Yeah. I heard the same. I figure maybe some of the stolen beefs find their way down there eventually, but there's some other place too, near at hand.'

'Any ideas?'

Sherman thought for a moment, inhaling deeply. 'I don't like to air any views without havin' proof, but my suspicions lie with a spread called the Scissors.'

'Come across it when I was ridin',' Kittredge said.

'It's owned by a man named Crudace.'

Kittredge looked up. 'Crudace? Would he have somethin' to do with the Crudace Land and Cattle Company? Saw the place in town.'

'Yeah, that's him.'

'I thought the name rang a bell. I been thinkin' about it but I can't place him. What makes you suspect him?'

Sherman shrugged. 'Ain't nothin' solid,' he said. 'In fact, ain't nothin' much at all, nothin' you could call evidence.'

He seemed reluctant to go on, so Kittredge encouraged him.

'Well, fact is I don't like his attitude to Miss Waggoner. Couple of times in town we ran across him. Kinda leery. I guess it made it worse that she seemed to encourage him.'

There was silence for a moment. A few of the horses shifted their feet. From inside the ranch house a door slammed.

'She's a strange girl,' Kittredge said. 'I can't make her out.'

Sherman breathed a cloud of blue smoke into the

40

air. 'She's a woman,' he answered. 'Don't try to figure her out.'

Kittredge threw a sidelong glance in the other man's direction. So Sherman had come under her spell too. He thought it might be a good idea to steer the conversation back in the direction of their previous exchange.

'This *hombre* Crudace. Wish I could remember where I've heard the name before. What do you know about him?'

'He's a pretty influential man around Arrowhead. Owns a lot of property in town and bought out the Scissors some time ago. He's a risin' star.'

Maybe it wasn't so surprising that Miss Trashy was prepared to flirt with him. A man like that could be an attractive proposition to an impressionable young girl. Or to a woman with an eye to the main chance.

'Seems to me there's only one way to put your suspicions to the test,' Kittredge said.

'Yeah. That's what I figure.'

'So why don't you and me take a ride and check out the Scissors?'

'Waggoner wouldn't like it. His policy so far has been to try and play down any differences between the Scissors and the Rafter W.'

'He don't have to like it. Especially if he didn't know anythin' about it.'

Sherman grinned. 'You're takin' a big chance for someone who just arrived on the scene.'

Kittredge shrugged.

'OK. Can't do no harm to check the place out,'

41

Sherman said.

'That's all I'm suggestin',' Kittredge replied.

There was silence between them for a few moments while they finished smoking their cigarettes. When they had ground them under heel Sherman turned to Kittredge.

'No time like the present,' he said.

Twenty minutes later they were heading out by the back of the corrals so as not to risk anyone seeing them, Kittredge riding the buckskin and Sherman a rangy Appaloosa. Clouds had come up from the west and it was a dark night. Their horses' hoofs beat a steady muffled tattoo but otherwise the range was silent. Only the occasional glint of a cow's horn or a few dim squatting shapes told of the presence of cattle, either singly or in little groups. It took them a considerable time to reach the limits of Rafter W land. After that there was a stretch of open range before they began to approach the Scissors, where they drew to a halt.

'Better take care from now on,' Sherman said. 'Take a look at that sign.'

Part of the range was fenced at this point and hanging low from an arched wooden structure was a board carrying the Scissors brand beneath which, in capital letters, was written:

TRESPASSERS WILL BE HANGED OR SHOT.
YOUR CHOICE.

'A mite unfriendly,' Kittredge commented.

42

'I reckon it means what it says.'

They touched their spurs to their horses' flanks and passed underneath the sign. After a time the land began to slope upwards to their left as it rose towards the low hills that they could see in the distance. Again they halted.

'Which way?' Kittredge said.

'I figure that if there's any rustled steers they'd be hidden away somewhere in those hills,' Sherman commented.

'Seems as good a place to start as any.'

As they progressed they came upon several groups of cattle. Each time Sherman swung down from the leather to take a look at the brand markings and each time it was the Scissors.

'The Rafter's quite a distinctive brand,' Kittredge said. 'So is the Scissors. Seems to me it'd be a pretty hard business to try and alter either one of 'em.'

'Get down and see this,' Sherman replied.

Kittredge slid from the saddle and bent down close to his comrade.

'Take a close look,' Sherman said.

Kittredge examined the brand in some detail before straightening up again.

'Cold brand,' he said.

'Yeah. I'd say it was put on through a wet blanket. That way it burns the hair down to the skin without actually scorchin' the hide. It's an old trick.'

'I don't get it. Why would Crudace want to brand his own cattle that way?'

Sherman was deep in thought. 'It would only make

sense if he wants to rebrand 'em. He's been puttin' pressure on the Rafter W for some time. It's no secret either that he's the rising man around here. What if he figures on gettin' control of the Rafter? Then he would simply be able to rebrand his cows with the Rafter brand.'

'I still don't see what he would get out of that.'

'Look at this cow. It ain't exactly in prime condition. The Rafter W has a reputation for raisin' the best beefs in the territory. He'd stand to make a lot more if he amalgamated his beefs with the Rafter's and put 'em on the market as one herd.'

Kittredge considered the proposition. 'I don't know,' he said. 'Seems to me there's a lot of ifs and maybes about it. Still, you're the ramrod. You know a lot better than me about these things.'

'Let's call it a workin' hypothesis.'

'What do we do now?'

Sherman thought for a moment. 'Let's carry on aways. See if we find anythin' else.'

'You mean some cow critter carryin' the Rafter Brand?'

'Anythin',' Sherman replied.

They mounted up and carried on riding in the direction of the hills. As they got higher they began to have a view of the surrounding country. At some distance away they eventually caught sight of a dim glow and then they could make out the ranchhouse. Lights were burning.

'Kinda lit up for this time of night,' Sherman commented. 'I wonder what's keepin' Crudace up so late.'

'Maybe we should ride over that way,' Kittredge replied. 'See if we can get up closer to the ranchhouse.'

'It's further off than it looks,' Sherman said.

Kittredge was about to reply when they both heard the sound of hoofbeats. They drew into the shelter of some trees and waited in silence. The hoofbeats grew louder, although they were still some distance away. The first light of a false dawn was lessening the gloom when they saw the shadowy shape of two riders pass by, heading in the direction of the ranchhouse.

'Some activity takin' place,' Sherman whispered.

'It might not mean anythin',' Kittredge responded.

'Sure.'

Sherman glanced up at the sky. 'I figure that's enough for one night,' he said. 'Won't be long till dawn. I reckon we'd best be headin' back.'

Kittredge nodded. Walking their horses out of cover, they turned and began to ride back in the direction of the Rafter W.

CHAPTER THREE

Sherman figured that Marshal Stegner had decided to do nothing further about the shoot-out at the Black Hat saloon. Some time had gone by since that affair so he was surprised when the marshal rode into the yard one morning.

'Howdy,' he said. 'Come to see Mr Waggoner?'

The marshal dismounted. 'Guess so, in a way. But it's you and the other fella I want to talk to really.'

Waggoner had appeared on the veranda. 'I heard that, Marshal,' he said. 'Hope my boys ain't been causin' any trouble. Why don't we all go inside and talk.'

The three men went into the ranch house.

'Like I say,' Waggoner resumed, 'I hope this ain't nothin' to do with any of my boys.'

The marshal looked from one to the other of them. Then his gaze rested on Sherman.

'This is kind of awkward,' he said. 'Fact of the matter is, Mr Crudace came to see me. He claims that two Rafter riders were seen on his property late on Tuesday night – Wednesday mornin', that is. He claims to have identified them as Sherman and the new fella – what's his name?'

'You mean Kittredge,' Waggoner interjected.

'Yeah, Kittredge.' He looked back at Sherman. 'Perhaps you could verify whether there is any truth in Crudace's assertion.'

Sherman glanced at Waggoner. 'Sorry, boss. I should have let you know.' He turned back to the marshal.

'It's true,' he said. 'Me and Kittredge did ride out that way. But we had a reason.'

'What was it?'

'Look, there's no secret about the fact that some of our cattle've been goin' missin'. The Scissors is the only other ranch in the neighbourhood. It's also no secret that Crudace would love to get his hands on the Rafter W.'

'It's true,' Waggoner said. 'On both counts.'

'Me and Kittredge just kinda figured it might be an idea to take a discreet look in the direction of the Scissors.'

'It weren't so discreet,' Waggoner murmured.

'And did you find anythin'?'

Sherman thought about the cold-branded cattle but decided to say nothing. His suspicions were too insubstantial.

'We saw a couple of riders,' he volunteered.

'Were you able to identify them?'

'Nope. But I figure they were Comancheros.'

'And have you any evidence to support that claim?'

'Nope. But you know yourself, Marshal, that some

47

pretty unsavoury characters have been takin' up residence in Arrowhead.'

Stegner was obviously uneasy. On the one hand he had known Waggoner and Sherman for a long time and knew they were solid citizens. What Sherman said was true; he had been having some trouble with outsiders recently. That was why he had taken a lenient view of the shoot-out in the first place. On the other hand, Sherman had admitted to trespassing on Crudace's range.

'Strictly speakin',' he said, 'I should take both you and Kittredge in. Where is Kittredge, by the way?'

'He's out fixin' some fencing,' Sherman replied.

'Like I say, I should be takin' you both in. But I figure you deserve a break.'

'Crudace certainly ain't goin' to see it that way.'

'I don't take orders from Crudace,' Stegner said. 'What Crudace thinks don't really concern me, even if he's got a case. Besides, I never liked him.'

Waggoner laughed. 'That's as good a reason as any,' he said, 'for stretchin' the law.'

The marshal gave him a stern look.

'Let's put it this way,' he said. 'I've done my duty comin' out here. It ain't my fault if neither Sherman nor Kittredge was available. It's no fault of mine that they were out brush-poppin' on some far flung corner of the range.'

Waggoner nodded. 'Sure appreciate your attitude,' he said.

The marshal turned to Sherman. 'As for that other matter, the witnesses confirm your story. As far as I'm

48

concerned, there's nothing more to be said.'

Sherman nodded.

'One word of warning. Watch your step with Crudace. He's a slippery character and he's sharp. I might not be able to give you another chance.'

The marshal turned to go. Waggoner and Sherman accompanied him outside. As Stegner mounted his horse Sherman looked up at an upstairs window and saw the face of Miss Trashy. It was only momentary, then the curtains twitched as she withdrew.

'Stay out of trouble,' the marshal said. 'Be seein' you.'

He settled himself in the saddle, then suddenly turned back.

'By the way,' he said. 'I almost forgot. There's a dance at the schoolhouse next Saturday night. I take it some of you boys will be there?'

'Sure thing,' Waggoner said. 'Ain't missed one yet.'

'Good, but remember what I say. Most of the Scissors boys are likely to be there too and I don't want any sort of trouble.'

'There won't be any, at least as not as far as the Rafter is concerned,' Waggoner said.

The marshal nodded, then rode away. Waggoner turned to his foreman.

'Listen to what he says,' he commented. There was a shadow of a grin across his features. 'And next time, make sure you let me know what you're doin'.'

They watched as the marshal disappeared from sight. Sherman walked away. There was one question burning in his mind. How did Crudace know about their night-time visit to the Scissors? It was extremely unlikely that anyone connected with the Scissors would have seen or recognized him or Kittredge. So where had Crudace got his information from?

The days passed. Work carried on about the ranch. Sherman mentioned the marshal's visit to Kittredge and voiced his concern about how Crudace had gained the information. Whatever thoughts each of them had on the matter, they remained for the moment unspoken. They talked about the forthcoming dance. At first Sherman was of the opinion that it might be wise if they both stayed away, but whatever the merits of that point of view neither of them gave it much consideration. Waggoner himself had not raised the matter and nobody wanted to miss the big social event. Although neither Sherman nor Kittredge would have admitted it, the prospect of seeing Miss Trashy at her finest and perhaps having a dance with her was the main attraction, even though, each in his own way, they no longer really considered the possibility of winning her. When the big day arrived, she certainly did not disappoint them.

For the occasion she had put on a plain white dress fastened at the waist with a blue ribbon. Her hair was done in ringlets, and round her neck she wore a necklace of pearls. The effect was simple but stunning. To convey her to town an almost brand-new surrey was employed, with her grandfather taking the role of driver. It had been polished up and there were rosettes on the horses' harnesses matching the blue of Miss

Trashy's sash.

Most of the ranch-hands were going to the dance and they had all put on their best duds. Some of them headed for town early, under strict instructions from Waggoner to behave themselves. By late afternoon the rest of them were ready and they set off for Arrowhead in high spirits. Sherman had put on a black suit with a matching waistcoat and string tie.

Kittredge was less stylishly attired. He had nothing other than the working apparel which he customarily wore and he had borrowed some items. He was slicked up in freshly washed blue jeans and a dark flannel shirt, loose and open at the neck. His boots were cleaned and he had decorated his hat with a band of woven horse-hair. It wasn't much of a concession to fashion but he still felt a little awkward. But what made him feel even more uncomfortable was the fact that he had to leave his guns behind. It was a convention that nobody went armed to these social events and Waggoner had insisted that everyone conform.

Outside the schoolhouse a number of wagons had already drawn up by the time Waggoner appeared. There were other surreys as well as buckboards and wagons. Saddle-horses were hitched to the schoolhouse fence. Inside, the school hall had been cleared of chairs, and benches had been pulled back against the walls. Already the place was busy. Some of the girls had seated themselves on the benches and children were running about. The first guests had arrived early to help with the food, which was set out on boards laid across boxes at the far end of the room. Coffee was already boiling in a big pot. The floor had been scrubbed and sprinkled with corn meal to make it smoother. As more people arrived groups gathered both inside the school and outside, exchanging range gossip and laughing and joking.

Waggoner brought the surrey to a halt, assisted his granddaughter to get down and together they walked into the hall. The timing was perfect. The hall had been rapidly filling with people and most of them looked up as Miss Trashy entered. Right behind them were some of the Rafter W cowboys, feeling constrained and self-conscious in their fancy shirts and freshly greased boots. Kittredge and Sherman remained outside, where knots of men stood talking and looked at the horses, checking to see how many of them carried the Scissors brand. To their surprise there were very few.

'Funny thing,' Sherman said. 'This kinda hoe-dig usually attracts folks from miles around.'

Kittredge looked about him. What Sherman said was evident in the numbers of people now beginning to enjoy themselves.

'Let's take a look inside,' he said.

The scene inside was very animated. People had gathered round the boards carrying the food and there was a lot of laughing, joshing and shouting. Occasionally a giggle from one of the girls would sound above the general hubbub at a joke some cowpoke had attempted. At the centre of a group of admirers Miss Trashy was holding court. Most of the people surrounding her were young men and Sherman suddenly felt his age.

'Recognize anyone?' Kittredge asked.

Sherman snapped back to attention. 'You mean from the Scissors?' Sherman's gaze swept the room. 'Nope,' he replied, 'but there's your friend Crudace over in the corner.'

Kittredge looked in the direction Sherman was indicating.

'Which one is he?' he asked.

'The tall fella with the slicked back hair and the fancy duds.'

Kittredge looked closely at the man. There was something about him that stirred his memory, something vaguely familiar. Suddenly he grinned.

'I remember now. I've come across Mr Crudace once before. Only in those days he wasn't any hot-shot rancher. He was a two-bit gambler workin' the river towns down St Louis way till he upset someone in a poker game and had to make a quick exit.'

Sherman looked up at his companion.

'Would that someone be you?' he asked.

Kittredge grinned. 'Coulda been. But it wasn't. Still, I figure that's the same *hombre*.'

Just then further conversation was interrupted by the strains of a fiddle being warmed up. Some of the people began to move in the fiddler's direction and he was quickly the centre of attraction. When he was ready the caller stepped into the room. He was a colourful individual, wearing a beaded vest over his bright-green shirt and a necklace studded with silver conches. At his appearance talking faded, then died away. People started backing towards the walls to make room for dancing.

Raising his head, the caller shouted: 'Podners to your puncheons'. The fiddler broke into a tune, beating time with his head and feet and, as people took to the floor, the voice of the caller rang out loud and clear:

Choose your podners, form a ring,
Figger eight and double L swing.

Most of the young men were timid at first but the whining of the fiddle, the scraping of high-heeled boots and the rhythmic shouts of the caller soon made them forget their skittishness. Some of the men wore a white handkerchief on their arms.

'What's the purpose of that?' Kittredge asked.

'Man, you been ridin' the trails too long,' Sherman replied. 'There's always more men than women at these shindigs. The ones wearing the handkerchiefs have agreed to take the lady's part.'

Kittredge rubbed his chin. 'Seems a mite odd,' he said.

'They get a reward. They get to sit with the ladies between dances.'

There was no fear of any of the ladies being ignored and soon the place was shaking as the feet of the dancers pounded the floor and the men swung the women in time to the shouted commands of the caller. Kittredge watched Miss Trashy, who was obviously the belle of the ball, as the particular section came to an end. Almost immediately the fiddler struck up another tune and the caller began again:

Ducks in the river, goin' to the ford,
Coffee in a little rag, sugar in the gourd.

Suddenly a figure appeared on the edge of the dance floor, pushing his way towards Miss Trashy. It was Crudace. Miss Trashy looked up and smiled at his arrival. It seemed to Kittredge that she was pleased to see him. The next moment she was dancing with him. Kittredge glanced at Sherman. His features were grim and his jaw was set. He made a move towards the dance floor but Kittredge held him by the arm.

'I don't know about you,' he said, 'but I figure I could do with a smoke.'

Sherman allowed himself to be led outside. Kittredge produced his pouch of Bull Durham and they rolled a couple of cigarettes. A few other men had drifted outside and some of them had bottles tilted to their mouths. There was a sound of galloping hoofs and some latecomers leaped from their saddles and stampeded into the school.

'That Crudace,' Sherman hissed. 'I don't know what Miss Trashy sees in him.'

'She don't see nothin' in him. She's just playin' the field.'

Sherman blew out a cloud of smoke and turned to the music.

'Are you OK?' Kittredge said.

Sherman nodded. They went back inside just as the tempo of the music changed to a Mexican-style rhythm. Suddenly Kittredge found himself next to Miss Trashy.

'Care to dance with me, Mr Kittredge?' she asked.

There was a mischievous look on her face. Looking up, Kittredge could see Crudace talking to a little group of older ladies. He turned his attention to his partner and led her on to the floor.

'You dance well,' she said.

'Better than Crudace?' Kittredge asked.

She glanced up at him from under lowered lashes.

'Really, Mr Kittredge, you mustn't concern yourself with Mr Crudace. He's just a neighbour.'

'That's not what Sherman seems to think.'

'Sherman has been in love with me since I was a girl. That's not my fault.'

Kittredge held Trashy at arm's length for a moment. There was a smile on her face and she was clearly relishing the whole situation. Suddenly he knew where Crudace had got his information about their nocturnal visit to the Scissors.

'You're quite a one,' he said.

The set ended and Waggoner appeared.

'You young ones having a good time?' he asked.

Kittredge nodded, made his way across to the coffee pot and helped himself to a cup. He looked for Sherman but couldn't see him. He was about to turn away when Crudace appeared at his elbow.

'I saw you dancin' with Miss Waggoner,' he said. 'Take my advice. Don't start gettin' ideas above your station.'

Kittredge threw him a cold glance.

'What's more,' Crudace continued, 'I fully intend to follow up on the little matter of you trespassin' on my land. If the marshal isn't prepared to do his job, I know somebody who will.'

'Are you threatenin' me?' asked Kittredge.

Crudace gave an ugly sneer. 'You'll see soon enough,' he said.

The lull which had ensued on the conclusion of the Spanish dance was broken by the caller's strident tones:

Come on, boys, and show some ditty,
Shake your feet and ketch your kitty.'

There was a movement towards the dance floor and Crudace was moving away when Kittredge seized the lapels of his jacket.

'I wouldn't do anything if I were you,' Crudace said with a leer.

Kittredge stiffened as he felt the barrel of a gun pressed against his back. He looked sideways and saw two ugly faces next to him.

'A word from me and he'll break your spine.'

Kittredge flexed and the gun was pressed harder into his back. Over Crudace's head Kittredge could see the dancers on the floor and other people standing and sitting round the periphery. Nobody had noticed that anything untoward was taking place.

'How come your cows is only hair-branded?' Kittredge said.

Crudace's lip curled in a gesture of anger.

'You better watch your mouth,' he hissed.

With a slight nod to his men, he turned and started to walk away. Kittredge felt the pressure on his back relent and when he turned there was only one retreating figure in sight. Kittredge made to go after him, then decided against it. He didn't want to cause a disturbance and besides, he was without his guns. He pushed his way past the dance floor where Miss Trashy was again the centre of attraction and made for the door. Sherman was standing outside. He looked up on Kittredge's arrival. Something about Kittredge's appearance made him raise an eyebrow.

'What happened to you?' he said.

Briefly, Kittredge outlined what had taken place, leaving out Crudace's references to Miss Trashy.

'You better watch your step,' Sherman said.

'I wish I had a gun,' Kittredge replied.

Sherman was quiet. From inside the schoolhouse the reel played by the violin and the stamping of feet mingled with the murmur of voices. A high-pitched voice yelled something.

'I'm still puzzlin' over why there ain't more of Crudace's men here,' Sherman said.

'Three's enough,' Kittredge commented.

'You didn't get a good look at any of 'em?'

Kittredge shook his head. He had only a blurred impression of two ugly faces and the third man, the one with the gun, he hadn't seen at all.

'There should be more,' Sherman mused, returning to his theme. 'Like I say, these hoe-digs is a big event. Folks don't miss it if they can help.'

The night wore on. People began to consider leaving. More men gathered outside, shouting and merry-making as they adjusted the saddles on their horses or hooked up their teams. Among the first to leave were Miss Trashy and her grandfather. As she passed Kittredge Miss Trashy gave him a look which he could not decipher. She took her seat in the surrey and her grandfather twitched the reins. A lot of the Rafter W riders remained behind.

Sherman and Kittredge mounted up and rode after the buggy. Behind them people were shouting their goodbyes and there was something of a kerfuffle as somebody tried to wrestle with a skittish team of horses that had been disturbed by all the noise. A few rigs swept past, their drivers keen to show that they were the quickest. Soon the town was left behind and they were alone at last on the trail back. The night was black and empty and made a strange contrast to everything that had gone before. Riding alongside Sherman, Kittredge began to feel solemn. Ahead of them the dark mass of the surrey could be dimly seen. They arrived at the fork and turned off the main trail. Now it was even darker and more silent. Here and there Kittredge could discern vague black shapes out on the range. At first he took no notice, knowing them to be cattle. There was something sinister about them, about the night; his horse sensed that something was amiss and its ears were pointed. It was Sherman who put a voice to his vague fears.

'Somethin's wrong,' he said.

Kittredge's nostrils smelt something in the air. It seemed that old Waggoner had sensed it too because the surrey had stopped and as they rode alongside he leaned out to speak to them.

'Go and check those cows,' he said.

Miss Trashy was looking anxious. She had thrown a cloak over her fineries and she was shivering a little although the night was warm.

'Wait here,' Sherman said. 'I'll take a look.'

He rode off. The others followed him with their eyes till he merged into the landscape. After a time the sound of hoofbeats told them he was returning. When he came alongside, even in the gloom, Waggoner could see that his face was taut and grim.

'The cows is dead,' he said. 'Somebody shot 'em.'

Miss Trashy gasped and Waggoner looked dumbfounded.

'Dead!' he exclaimed. 'How many of 'em?'

'All the ones I checked on so far.'

A sudden thought came to Kittredge. 'Better get back to the ranch,' he said.

Nobody needed to ask any questions. They knew the dread that was in his mind.

'You two ride on ahead,' Waggoner said. 'We'll be right behind you.'

Sherman hesitated. 'Will you and Miss Trashy be safe. . . ?' he began.

'Just do it!' Waggoner shouted.

He raised his whip and cracked it across the backs of the horses. The buggy lurched forward. Sherman gave Kittredge a bemused look.

'I'll keep an eye on the surrey,' Kittredge said.

With a muffled thanks Sherman dug his spurs into the Appaloosa's side and set off at a gallop for the ranch house. Whatever Waggoner thought of the matter, he did not stop the surrey to expostulate. Instead he carried on at what Kittredge considered a dangerous pace. They weren't far from the ranch house when they saw Sherman riding back towards them. The surrey drew to a shuddering halt as Sherman and Kittredge came alongside.

'Well!' Waggoner shouted.

'It ain't good,' Sherman said. 'Two of the boys have been killed and the ranch has been ransacked.'

'What!'

'I'm sorry, Mr Waggoner. The ranch house has been ransacked. I don't know if anythin's been took, but whoever it was done a pretty good wreckin' job.'

Without waiting for further description, Waggoner whipped up the horses and they all set off pell-mell to cover the remaining distance to the ranch. Immediately they pulled in they could see a body in the yard. The second was lying in a stream of light falling through the open door of the ranch house. When they stepped inside they saw the damage which had been wrought: tables and chairs toppled over, ornaments spilled across the floor, curtains ripped from their hangings. Waggoner stomped across the broken shards of glass and crockery into the other rooms but to his surprise and relief the damage seemed to have been confined to the main room.

'Why would anyone do this?' he yelled.

Miss Trashy had turned to Kittredge and was leaning on his arm, sobbing.

'I don't know,' Sherman said. 'But it looks like they came in shootin'.'

Apart from the evidence of the bodies outside, there

were bullet holes in the walls and ceiling.

'I wonder how many cows they slaughtered?' Waggoner said. 'We'll have to leave it till mornin' to take a good look.'

He walked across to where the cabinet containing his drinks had been wrenched off the wall. Bottles lay in a mashed heap and a smell of liquor filled the air.

'Patricia,' he said. 'Why don't you make us some coffee?'

Miss Trashy looked anxiously towards the kitchen.

''It's all right,' her grandfather assured her. 'There's nobody here and as far as I can see they ain't disturbed anywhere else.'

Sherman glanced towards the stairs. 'I'll go take a look up there,' he said. In a few moments he was back. 'No damage that I can see,' he confirmed.

'Well,' Waggoner replied. 'I guess we can be thankful that the damage wasn't even worse.'

For a few minutes the men busied themselves trying to restore the place to a semblance of its former appearance. As they were doing so Miss Trashy appeared with the coffee.

'Sorry I can't offer anything stronger,' Waggoner said. They sat down and Miss Trashy poured.

'What do you make of it?' Waggoner said, addressing them generally.

They looked at one another. Miss Trashy began to sob again. Sherman put down his coffee cup.

'Coulda been anybody,' he said.

'More likely someone with a grudge,' Waggoner replied.

'Yeah,' Sherman said.

There was a pause. Outside the horses snickered. Kittredge got to his feet.

'The remuda,' he said.

In an instant he was running towards the corrals, aware for the first time of the silence. One of the corral gates was ajar and some of the horses were missing but most of them were still there. Quickly, he made his way back.

'It mighta been worse,' he said. 'I figure it this way. Whoever it was came in with the intention of causin' maximum damage. They butchered any cattle they came across. They probably shot one of those men outside as they rode into the yard. Then they were disturbed by the other one. They killed him too and decided to make their getaway. On the way out they loosed the missin' horses.'

'Looks that way,' Waggoner said. 'Still don't make much sense.'

Sherman shot Kittredge a glance. 'Me an' Kittredge noticed there weren't too many Scissors riders out to the dance tonight,' he remarked.

'So? What are you sayin'?'

Sherman shuffled as Miss Trashy gave him a look.

'I don't want to say anythin' because there ain't no proof. We're talkin' generally here. But I been askin' myself why those Scissors boys would give the dance a miss.'

'What?' Waggoner said. 'Are you implyin' that they might have had somethin' to do with this?'

'I'm just sayin' it's maybe worth considerin'. The

63

Scissors boys weren't at the hoe-dig like you'd expect. People would know that the Rafter would be kinda light on numbers.'

Miss Trashy suddenly looked angry. 'Are you trying to insinuate that Mr Crudace might have had something to do with this?' she exclaimed.

Sherman looked helpless beneath her withering gaze. 'I'm just sayin',' he began when Kittredge interrupted.

'Sherman's got a point. We were talkin' about the absence of Scissors men at the dance. This could be one explanation.'

Waggoner put his hand on his granddaughter's shoulders but she shook him off. In one bound she had left her seat and was rushing for the stairs. Kittredge made a move in her direction.

'Leave her,' Waggoner said. 'She's obviously upset about everythin' that's happened. Give her some time to herself.'

Kittredge resumed his seat and took another sip of coffee.

'It's true that things ain't been good recently between the Scissors and the Rafter W,' Waggoner mused. Suddenly he was angry too. 'By all that's holy,' he hissed, 'if I find that there's any substance to your suppositions, I'll make Crudace pay.'

After his outburst they sat in silence for a time before Kittredge spoke.

'There ain't much we can do at the moment,' he said, 'other than to carry on tryin' to tidy up around here. Tomorrow we'll look for any clues and some of the boys can ride out and see about bringin' in those missin' broncs. Me and Sherman can take a look around and see just what the damage is in dead stock.'

Waggoner looked towards the doorway. 'Where are the rest of the hands?' he said. 'Some of 'em should be back by now.'

'They'll be gettin' back soon,' Sherman said. 'I reckon we should move those bodies into the barn until we can get the undertaker to come out tomorrow.'

Just as they had finished carrying out the task the first riders began to come in. They were still merry and some of them had had too much to drink. Sherman told them to get into the bunkhouse and settle down for the rest of the night, not wanting to go into any explanations for the moment. Whether or not they noticed that anything was amiss it was hard to say.

For his part, Kittredge gave further thought to his encounter with Crudace and his hardcases at the hoe-dig. He, for one, was pretty convinced that the land agent lay behind events. One thing he and Sherman had noticed, and that was that the man who had been shot on the veranda had fired a couple of rounds himself.

The next morning it became clear that he had succeeded in wounding one of his attackers. A trail of blood led away from the veranda and round the corner of the ranch house. It was clear that the man had succeeded in mounting his horse at this point and from the evidence of the sign that the attackers had left it seemed there might be as many as a dozen of them. Whoever they were, they didn't seem to be too bothered about leaving a trail behind.

Leaving Sherman to check on the situation with the cattle, Kittredge followed the sign. At intervals there were spots of dried blood on the grass and at one point it appeared that at least two of the riders had drawn to a halt. There was more blood on the grass, then it seemed to disappear. The man must have received some attention and the flow of blood had been temporarily stanched.

The trail led, not as Kittredge had expected, in the direction of the Scissors, but in precisely the opposite direction, towards the rough country and the badlands to the south.

After riding for a good long time Kittredge saw something on the ground ahead of him round which a swarm of flies was buzzing. Carefully, he drew his Colt from its holster, got down from the buckskin and cautiously approached the object. As he got closer he saw it was the body of a man, lying on his side, and Kittredge knew he was dead. Keeping alert, Kittredge dropped down on one knee and turned the man over. He had been shot in the chest and a crude attempt had been made to bandage up the wound. Kittredge looked closely at the man's unkempt and pointed features and at his worn, dusty attire. He wore a grimy black-leather jacket over a silk shirt and though someone had removed his gunbelt it was obvious that he was no cowpuncher.

'Comanchero,' Kittredge muttered.

The fact that the man was no range rider did not cause Kittredge to exonerate Crudace from any blame concerning the attack on the ranch. Rather the question that rose in Kittredge's mind was: what was the connection between Crudace and the Comancheros? And what was the name that old quack Grattan had mentioned to him, the name of the man he had been advised to avoid? El Serpiente. Maybe the time was fast coming when he would need to pay a visit to the Spanish Bit.

CHAPTER FOUR

Several days after the hoe-dig Cass Grattan's wagon came trundling down the main street of Arrowhead. People passing on the boardwalks looked up as it lumbered by, some of them taking the time to wave to the oldster sitting on the driving seat. To the older folks especially he was a familiar figure who came and went on a fairly regular basis. Marshal Stegner came out of his office as the wagon came alongside.

'Figure to put on a show?' he asked.

'Well, Marshal, I guess that mainly depends on you.'

The marshal laughed. 'Just so long as you don't cause no disturbance,' he said.

Grattan flicked the reins and the wagon rolled on, eventually coming to a halt in the town square. Grattan looked about him. It was still quite early but he wasn't one to waste an opportunity. He climbed down and moved to the back of the wagon, where he undid the canvas strings. He pulled the canvas awning aside, then carried out a table on which he set up some of his bottles of medicine. People were already stopping to see what was going on and presently he began to address them.

'Folks, I can tell that some of you have been havin' a hard time. I can see from the look in your eyes that you been afflicted. Times is hard and there ain't no allowin' for the aches and pains and natural shocks that flesh is heir to. Where are you goin' to find respite? Where are you gonna find strength to carry on day after day, doin' the things you gotta do, carryin' out the daily tasks the Lord has allotted you. And where are you gonna find a cure when the mad dog bites, when the fever strikes, when the ague creeps up on you and turns your bones into water?

'I don't need to tell you; you all know what I'm talkin' about. I'm talkin' about Doctor Grattan's all-purpose, cure-all elixir, the elixir of strength and renewal, the elixir it took years of research and knowl-edge to distil.'

He looked about. A sizeable crowd had gathered and he wished he had someone on hand to act as his stooge. But he had no one. Maybe he should have taken the time to set things up properly, but it was a situation he had been in many times before and he knew how to influ-ence a crowd. He held up one of his medicine bottles.

'Here it is, folks, the water of life, the nectar of the gods, the secret of the ancients rediscovered. Here it is, the cure for all your complaints. So you have a bad back; the medicine will relieve it. So you have stom-achache; put aside the peppermint oil and take the real soother. So you have inflammation and sprains; here is the genuine knitbone. It don't matter what the com-plaint is: rheumatism, septic wounds, snakebite, ulcers, abscesses, mere boils and bruises; your worries, your fears, your sufferings are at an end.'

Somebody in the crowd shouted something and a ripple of laughter passed round. It didn't faze the old quack; a response was what he had been looking for.

'Step forward, friend. Don't be shy, step up and speak your mind. You have doubts? You're not alone. But I ask you to cast your doubts aside just long enough to allow the truth to shine forth. As the good book says, only believe. Only believe, my friend, and the truth will appear and the truth shall set you free.'

Grattan's choice of words was deliberate; it didn't matter if the language was vague. It suited his purposes to give it an imprecise religious tone. Now he could begin to whip the crowd into a kind of emotional fervour so that the people wouldn't be too sure whether it was their physical ailments or their spiritual infirmities he had come to cure.

'Friends, the time is at hand. The time it is today. For long years I have travelled the dusty roads, wandered the highways and byways, always working to develop the liquid ambrosia which is now yours to obtain. Yours to reap the benefits. Never again need you—'

Suddenly his words were cut short as a shot rang out and the bottle he was holding aloft shattered into fragments. There was a united gasp from the crowd and then another burst of laughter. Grattan was too startled to realize what had happened till a flow of blood down his arm brought the awareness that he had been cut by a shard of glass. He swung his head, encompassing the crowd in a sweeping glance, but he couldn't see where

70

the shot had come from. While some of the braver elements continued to observe him, most of the crowd was beginning to disperse.

One man stepped forward and, as if by accident, stumbled into the table on which Grattan had placed his wares. The table went over with a crash and the bottles of medicine smashed into fragments, pouring their contents into the dust.

'Sorry!' The man laughed.

His face was distorted in an ugly leer as he brushed past the startled showman. Grattan watched him disappear down an alley before facing the rapidly disappearing crowd. After a moment he felt a hand on his shoulder.

'Thought I told you not to cause any trouble.' Grattan turned to face the marshal.

There was a grin on the lawman's face. 'Guess it weren't the response you were lookin' for. Let me give you a hand to tidy things up.'

Stegner noticed the blood running down Grattan's arm. 'I'll get the doc,' he said.

He strode off and came back a short time later with the doctor.

'It's nothin' but a scratch,' Grattan remarked.

'I've got the deputy checkin' to see if he can discover who fired the shot,' Stegner said. 'But I don't expect to get a result.'

Grattan nodded. 'Coulda come from anywhere,' he said.

The marshal looked up at the surrounding buildings. From an open upstairs window overlooking the square a curtain fluttered.

71

'Reckon it probably came from up there,' he said. 'Whoever it was, he was lookin' to have him some fun. He was a good shot. If he'd intended anythin' worse you wouldn't be here.'

'Comes with the territory,' Grattan responded.

'Come on over to my office and have a drink,' the marshal said. 'You too, Doc.'

It was evening by the time Grattan eventually settled down to camp in a grove of trees not far outside town. The marshal's whiskey followed by a subsequent visit to the Black Hat saloon had helped put a gloss on the affair and he was feeling a lot more positive about things as he unhitched the mules from the wagon and set about building a fire. Maybe he would try something different next time. Maybe a little dramatic entertainment would go down better with the good citizens of Arrowhead; a Shakespearian interlude perhaps. Or possibly a bit of preaching. He would think about it.

He would also think about what form of revenge he might be able to exact on the man who had knocked over his table. He had recognized him as one of the Comancheros he had traded with. It was a fair bet that the man who had shot the bottle out of his hand and injured his arm was one of them too. The window the marshal had drawn his attention to was in the Crudace Land and Cattle Company building. Now what would some gunslick be doing there?

Kittredge returned to the Rafter W to find that Sherman and some of the cowhands had completed their assessment of the damage which had been done to the livestock.

About forty head of cattle had been slaughtered.

'I figured to sell 'em at a little less than twenty dollars a head,' Waggoner said. 'That's a loss of eight hundred dollars.'

'That's a lot of money,' Sherman remarked.

'Maybe we should bring the marshal in on this,' Sherman said. 'Let him know our suspicions about Crudace and the Scissors.'

Waggoner thought about it. 'I don't know,' he said. 'I don't like to impose on him. Remember he was pretty good about that little matter of trespassin'.'

'If only we had more definite proof of Crudace's involvement.'

Kittredge looked up. 'Maybe there's another way of gettin' it,' he said. He explained about the body he had discovered.

'Whoever else from the Scissors might have been involved,' he said, 'it seems to me like Crudace is gettin' help from the Comancheros. We didn't find no evidence of any Rafter W stock on Crudace's property.'

'We didn't get much chance to find out,' Sherman remarked.

He looked at Kittredge and there was an unspoken meaning in his glance. Both of them had their suspicions about who had been involved in informing Crudace about that night's escapade but neither wanted to be the first to mention the name of Miss Trashy. Especially to her grandfather's face.

'We know damn well that some of the stock has been run off, quite apart from what happened on the night of the dance. What about that other ranch, the Spanish

Bit? Some folks say it's run by the Comancheros. What if the missin' cattle are there rather than the Scissors? And what if there's a connection between the Spanish Bit and Crudace?'

Waggoner thought hard. 'Hell, you got a point,' he exclaimed. 'In fact, it might not be a bad idea if I was to do some checkin' in town on who owns the deeds to the Spanish Bit.'

'That could be difficult,' Sherman said. 'If Crudace is involved, even to the extent of havin' a stake in it, you can be sure he would take care to cover his tracks.'

'He ain't runnin' that Land and Cattle Company for nothin',' Kittredge said. 'It would give him the inside track to pickin' up a spread like the Spanish Bit as well as the means to keep it concealed.'

'OK,' Waggoner said. 'So what are you proposin', Kittredge?'

'I'm proposin' that me and Sherman take a ride down through the badlands and take a look at the Spanish Bit.'

'Like you did with the Scissors?'

Kittredge and Sherman again exchanged glances.

'This time it's got to be kept secret. That should be a lot easier because the Spanish Bit is a long ways off. I don't know how Crudace found out about our visit to the Scissors, but this is a whole different situation. Anyone might be able to see that we're gone, but it's not likely anybody would guess where.'

'Unless they get on to you quick and track you there,' Waggoner said.

Kittredge shrugged. 'Like I say, it ain't likely, but it's

a risk we'll just have to take.'

Sherman nodded. 'I think Kittredge is right,' he said. 'We'll need to keep this thing top secret and not tell no one.'

'Yeah, the fewer people know what's goin' on the better,' Kittredge added. 'In fact, it's better if no one knows anythin' about it.' He paused. 'Not even Brigstock or any other of the hands. Even if you're sure you can trust them.'

Sherman caught a quick glance from Kittredge. 'Not even Miss Trashy,' he said.

Waggoner shook his head. 'I think you're being a bit dramatic. I appreciate the need to keep things under wraps, but don't you think you might be overstating the case just a little?'

'Maybe so,' Kittredge said, 'but it's better that way.'

'OK, whatever you say,' Waggoner said. 'Now just when do you intend goin'?'

'Tomorrow,' Kittredge replied. 'There ain't no rush to get there, but I figure it might be worth checkin' things out on the way.'

'What? You figure there might be rustled stock hidden someplace else?'

'It's a possibility. We can keep a lookout just in case.'

'And what do you intend doing when you get there? Always assuming you find something suspicious going on.'

Kittredge rubbed his chin. He broke into a laugh and he could see that Sherman was grinning too.

'Shucks. Can't say as I've thought that far ahead.'

'Well,' Waggoner concluded, 'I guess you'll both

have plenty of time to figure something on the way.'

In fact the trip was delayed for a few days by another appearance from the marshal. The bodies of the two men had been delivered to the coroner and, despite his reluctance to involve Stegner, Waggoner had to make some explanations. He didn't mention anything about Crudace, contenting himself with saying that it seemed to be the work of some of the Comancheros who had been seen around Arrowhead of late. The marshal was sympathetic and appeared to agree with Waggoner's conclusion.

'I tell you what,' he remarked. 'I'm startin' to get a mite worried about those *hombres*. Things quieted down some after that incident with Sherman and Kittredge, but they've got a bit spicy again just lately. If this is part of the pattern, the stakes are risin'.'

He told Waggoner about some of the things which had been taking place, minor matters mostly like the incident involving Grattan, but all tending in the same direction.

'Arrowhead ain't what it was. Still, I guess it's my business to keep things from gettin' out of hand. You don't fancy bein' a deputy?'

Waggoner laughed.

'Well, it might come down to it in the end,' the marshal said. 'By the way, there's still some little details connected with the trespassin' charge to be cleared up, so tell Sherman and Kittredge to stick around for just another day or two in case I need them. I don't like that slippery snake Crudace one bit, but I guess we got to follow the protocol.'

76

While they were waiting for clearance from the marshal Sherman and Kittredge got on with some of the basic ranch work that required doing. In the days following the hoe-dig neither of them had seen very much of Miss Trashy. One morning she went off riding in the company of Brigstock and returned a couple of hours later. Kittredge was completing work on fixing the corral when they came by but Miss Trashy very pointedly ignored him. Brigstock gave him a backward glance and Kittredge suddenly felt himself wondering whether Brigstock might be the go-between for Miss Trashy and Crudace. He was loath to think so because from what contact he'd had with the man, he quite liked him.

That was one of the troubling aspects of the situation. The shadow of suspicion hung over things and would continue to do so while matters remained unresolved. It would be good to get away to the Spanish Bit. Maybe things would become a lot clearer after that, although neither he nor Sherman had much idea about what they were to do once they got there or in what shape a resolution might appear.

It was a relief to them when Stegner at last gave them the all clear. How far Crudace had intended to take the trespass affair Waggoner had no way of knowing, but he suspected that the marshal was responsible in no small manner for thwarting him. The following morning, just as dawn was breaking, Kittredge and Sherman slipped unobtrusively away from the Rafter W.

A long way further south, El Serpiente was also thinking about the Spanish Bit. He had spent a long time in his mountain fastness considering his situation and he had at last come to a decision. If he was to break free of Crudace and assert his independence of that gringo dog, now was the time to do it. All the time he had been doing Crudace's dirty business he had been steadily building up his own power and reputation. Now he felt that the balance of forces had swung in his direction as far as it was likely to do so.

The final objective would be to take over the Scissors and establish himself as a respectable landowner and rancher where the real pickings were to be had, which was one reason he had been prepared to fall in with Crudace's wishes and send some of his men up there to apply pressure to rival spreads like the Rafter W. Who could say? Maybe the Rafter W would fall into his own hands eventually, like a ripe plum.

His first target, though, was the Spanish Bit. He was probably still outnumbered and outgunned by Crudace's gang of cowpokes and hardcases running the ranch, but they would have no reason to suspect him. He was fairly free to come and go at the Spanish Bit. He had become a familiar sight riding in with stolen and bartered cattle for Crudace, and Crudace's men would have no reason to expect that anything had changed.

Right now, however, there was Carmelita. She was getting too full of herself. The time had come to teach her a lesson. It wouldn't be the first. He felt a prick of desire as he heard her move about in the adjoining room. He put down the bottle of tequila he was drinking from, got to his feet and stepped to the door. Carmelita had been cooking and she leaned against a bench, looking up as he entered the room. Sweat trickled down from her neck and stood out against the soft brown flesh of her chest. Her dress clung to her as she moved forward and he pushed her back. He put his arm around her neck and pulled her to him, but before he could kiss her she pushed him away.

'Not now,' she said.

He grabbed her once more but again she avoided him. He lifted his hand and struck her heavily across the mouth. Blood flowed from a corner of her lips and it seemed to inflame him further. Doubling his fist, he struck her again on the cheek and she fell to one knee, looking up at him with hatred in her eyes. Before she could do anything to avoid him, he followed up his attack with a kick to the stomach and as she fell forward, gasping with pain, he picked her up in his strong arms and carried her through to the bedroom.

'It's time you learned obedience,' he snarled.

He struck her again and then, unbuttoning his trousers, he forced her down on the bed, tearing her blouse and pressing his hand hard on her breast. For a few moments she continued to struggle; then, as another punch rocked her head backwards, she lay inert while he did what he wanted.

When it was finished she lay for a long time, pain racking her body. After a time she became aware of sounds outside, then the light began to dwindle. She dragged herself to her feet, splashed some water across her face from a bowl standing on a dresser and then, with some difficulty, changed her clothes. She knew from previous experience that once Gonsalez had had his way with her, he made himself scarce, going off to drink and gamble with some of his cronies.

Peering from the doorway of the stone house, she saw that the platform outside was deserted and that night was rapidly falling. She continued watching for a little while longer before going back inside, re-emerging carrying a rifle and a pack slung across her shoulders.

Then she started on the precarious track leading down to the canyon floor. At the bottom she paused for breath before making for the horses grazing the grass which grew near the stream. Near by was a rough shed in which some saddles hung on hooks. She took one, fastened it to the back of a piebald palomino, and started to lead the horse along the winding path leading out of the mesa. Now and again she looked back anxiously but there was no sign of Gonsalez.

By the time she came through the narrow entrance and emerged on to the open plain, darkness had fallen. She climbed awkwardly into the saddle and began to ride away into the night.

Kittredge and Sherman were in no hurry to get to the Spanish Bit. Kittredge didn't think it likely that the stolen cattle would be found anywhere else but at the ranch, but they were keeping an eye open as they rode. Besides, it made sense to keep their horses fresh. They made their slow way through the rangelands, watching for sign and circling, taking in more territory than they would by a more direct route. They saw some old buffalo trails but nothing more significant.

'If the Comancheros are drivin' longhorns down this way, they sure know how to keep it a secret,' Kittredge commented.

'It's a big country,' Sherman replied. 'Figure I'd be more surprised if we found any traces.'

Days passed, and then they were in harsh, broken terrain which gradually became drier and more rugged. Pinnacles of red rock reached bony fingers and stark tablelands loomed against the brassy sky. Pulling to a halt, Kittredge reached for his field glasses.

'Seen somethin'?' Sherman asked.

Kittredge was scanning their back trail. Presently he detected a faint dark patch on the horizon. He handed the glasses to his companion.

'Probably just a dust devil,' Sherman remarked.

'Or somebody comin' after us,' Kittredge replied.

'Who would know we're here?'

Kittredge shrugged his shoulders.

'Probably not,' Sherman said. 'How many, do you reckon?'

'A few,' Kittredge replied.

They rode on, keeping a close eye for signs of pursuit but there was no further indication of anything untoward. The sun burned down on them and they were caked with dust. Heat waves danced in the air. After a time they stopped again to take a drink and wash out the mouths and nostrils of their horses with a wet sponge. They moved on slowly till the declining sun told them it was time to find somewhere to camp.

They found a clump of brush in a hollow, at the bottom of which was a small seep partly concealed by

81

undergrowth. They unsaddled the horses and picketed them before building a fire, calculating that they were well enough hidden for the flames not to be detected. They cooked beans and bacon and Kittredge filled the coffee pot with water from the sump. It was brackish and alkaline but it served its purpose. When they had eaten Sherman sat back and built himself a smoke, offering his pouch to Kittredge.

'I don't like to bring this up,' he said, 'but just what do we intend doin' once we reach the Spanish Bit?'

Kittredge rolled himself a thin cigarette. 'I been puzzlin' about it,' he said.

'And what have you come up with?'

Kittredge looked at Sherman though a haze of smoke.

'I been thinkin' about that dust cloud. If it's some of Crudace's men, they know who we are and they know where we're headed. Seems to me that a change of plan might be called for.'

'What you got in mind?'

'Ever hear of an *hombre* called El Serpiente? Leastways that's the name he likes to go by. Apparently his real name is Gonsalez.'

Sherman's brows were creased in thought. 'Now you mention it, yeah. Might even have said somethin' to you. Where else did you hear about him?'

'Your friend and mine, Grattan. I told you how I came across Grattan while I was soundin' out the territory. He warned me about Gonsalez. Figures he's the leader of the Comancheros. To cut a long story short, we know there's a connection between the

82

Comancheros and Crudace. We didn't find no trace of our cattle at the Scissors, so it's a fair guess that they're at the Spanish Bit. Seems to me like it might be a more sensible idea to find out where this Gonsalez is based and find out just what the score is.'

'Wouldn't he be at the Spanish Bit?'

'I'd be willin' to bet the Spanish Bit is run by Crudace. Crudace has been usin' his contacts with the Comancheros to stir up trouble for Waggoner. So ask yourself this question. What does Gonsalez get out of it?'

'I don't follow.'

'Gonsalez might once have been a two-bit owlhoot willin' to offer his services to Crudace. But if what Grattan said is to be believed, he's a lot more than that now. So why would he be doin' Crudace's dirty work? It don't make sense unless he's got plans of his own to take over from Crudace, not only the Spanish Bit but the whole kit and caboodle. The Scissors too. Maybe it was Gonsalez who cold branded those cow critters.'

'I think I see what you're drivin' at.'

'If there's someone on our trail, and assuming they're Crudace's boys, we'd be walkin' straight into a trap if we turned up at the Spanish Bit. So why not get straight to Gonsalez?'

Sherman poured another cup of coffee. 'Hell,' he commented, 'That sure don't taste so good.'

'It's hot and it's strong,' Kittredge said. 'I've drunk a lot worse.'

Sherman's face was twisted in a grimace of distaste but he carried on swallowing.

'I tell you what,' he said. 'It seems a pity to have come all this way and not at least pay a visit to the Spanish Bit. Why don't we do like we did with the Scissors and kind of check it out on the way by? I'd sure be interested to see just what stock they got there. Who knows, we might even pick up some clue as to where to find Gonsalez.'

'Good idea. Maybe we could swing by. If Gonsalez has been drivin' cattle, there's a chance we might find sign that would lead us to where he might be holed up.'

Sherman grinned. 'The way we're beginnin' to look,' he said, glancing at Kittredge's growth of beard and their travel-worn gear, 'I figure we could be taken for a couple of Comancheros any time.'

It was late. Sherman moved off to take the first watch, leaving Kittredge to grab a little sleep. Taking his Winchester, he moved up to the edge of the depression where they had set their camp to a spot which gave him a decent view of the desert they had come across. In the moonlight the place looked even more strange and unearthly than it did by day. The cacti laid weird shadows on the scrub and sand and the cholla needles seemed to glow with a pale white phosphorescence. A bat fluttering near by only seemed to intensify the silence which hung like a physical presence over the alien land. It was a silence that seemed pregnant with a latent possibility and Sherman found himself listening to it, listening to the silence.

Then he heard a faint sound, like the gentle trickle of sand. He tensed, straining his ears and looking into the far distance. He expected that whatever it was must be a long way off, possibly a distant rider, so that he was

84

taken completely by surprise when a dark shape suddenly loomed up before him. Then a sharp stab of pain in his shoulder brought awareness and he managed to roll to one side as the shadowy figure landed on top of him.

His rifle slipped from his fingers as something glinted in the moonlight and a knife descended towards him. Just in time he reached up his hand to grip his attacker's wrist. Twisting his other shoulder, he kicked out and succeeded in unseating his opponent so that they both went rolling over and the knife fell to the floor. In an instant he was on his feet and as the other figure sought to do likewise he kicked out hard and caught his attacker on the neck. There was a gasp of pain and then a spluttering cough as the person struggled for breath. Without hesitation he kicked out again and the figure went sprawling. He reached down for the rifle and pointed it at his assailant's head.

'Get up!' he hissed.

There was no response and he realized that whoever it was, was unconscious. Carefully he knelt down and turned the figure over. As soon as the moonlight fell on its features he gave a little gasp.

'It's a woman!' he breathed.

There was a movement behind him and he spun round but it was only Kittredge with his Colt in his hand.

'Thought I heard somethin',' he said.

Sherman was breathless. He pointed to the figure on the ground. Kittredge bent to look closer and gave out a low whistling sound.

'Now what in tarnation could she be doin' here?'

'I don't know,' Sherman gasped, 'but she pretty nigh killed me.'

He became aware that he was bleeding. The woman's knife had sliced through his jacket and cut him across the shoulder.

'I don't think it's bad,' Sherman said.

'Let's get her to the camp,' Kittredge replied. 'Then we can bandage you up.'

They lifted the unconscious woman and carried her back. The fire had sunk low and Kittredge threw some brush on to it. It blazed up and at that moment the woman opened her eyes. She looked about confusedly before her glance fell on the two men and the barrel of Kittredge's six-gun.

'You kill me?' she said.

Sherman reached out and poured a cup of coffee. 'Here, drink this,' he said.

She looked aggressively from one to the other, then she noticed the blood staining Sherman's shirtfront.

'I have medicine,' she said. 'Herbs. In saddle-bags.'

Kittredge looked at Sherman.

'You show me,' he said.

'Watch what you're doin',' Sherman advised. 'It could be a trap.'

Kittredge nodded to the woman and she got to her feet.

'Don't make any false moves,' Kittredge said. He kept the gun trained on her back as she began to move away, walking up to the rim of the hollow and then following a track through the brush. It seemed to

Kittredge that they were walking for some time and he was beginning to feel that he had made a wrong move when he saw a horse outlined against the skyline. She went up to it, whispering softly.

'Take it easy,' Kittredge said.

'The medicine is in the saddle-bags,' she replied.

'Bring the horse,' Kittredge said.

The horse was loosely tied. In a few moments they were walking slowly back towards the camp. As they did so Kittredge had a sudden misgiving. Had it been sensible to leave Sherman behind? But Sherman could look after himself, wounded or not. He hadn't needed to worry, because when they got back Sherman was sitting by the fire with his rifle across his knees and a cigarette in his mouth. As the woman approached he held out his tobacco pouch.

'You want a cigarette?' he asked.

The woman looked hesitant, then nodded her head. While Kittredge rolled a smoke she took something from a bundle and began cleaning Sherman's wound, wiping something over it.

'What is it?' Sherman asked.

She did not reply but went on with her ministrations. As she did so Sherman looked at her more closely. She had long dark hair which hung over her shoulder. Her blouse had been ripped, presumably during the struggle he had had with her, to reveal the swell of the upper part of her breasts. Catching his involuntary glance, she pulled the blouse together. For a moment their eyes met. Hers were large and dark and for a fraction of a second he thought he read tenderness in them before they reverted to being blank. As far as either Sherman or Kittredge could make out, she was packing the wound with a kind of poultice made of leaves or grass. Although it hurt, her touch was light and deft.

When she had finished she sat back and took the cigarette Kittredge proffered her. Kittredge had another inspiration.

'Are you hungry?' he asked.

The woman did not reply but Kittredge had a feeling that she hadn't eaten for some time. He threw some bacon into the pan and placed it over the flames. When it was ready she seemed willing enough to eat it but she remained silent. The situation was awkward but both Kittredge and Sherman felt instinctively that the best thing would be to make it clear to the woman that they meant her no harm, and to hope that they might win her trust.

For the rest of the night they remained in silence. Occasionally Kittredge replenished the fire and the last time he did so the woman seemed to have fallen asleep. She showed no sign of remorse for her action in stabbing Sherman or any sign of apprehension about her situation.

At long last the eastern sky began to lighten. There was a chill in the air and Kittredge placed a blanket round the sleeping woman. As he did so he felt Sherman's eyes on him.

'Who do you reckon she is?' he said.

'Guess we'll find out soon enough.'

'She's mighty pretty,' Sherman added.

'How's the shoulder?'

Sherman reached a hand up to the wound. 'You know, I'd almost forgotten about it.'

As dawn broke Kittredge fed some more sticks on to the ashes of the fire and made breakfast. The woman was awake but did not move. After they had all eaten Kittredge and Sherman went to see to the horses. When they returned the woman had washed their dishes. For the first time they noticed that her face was bruised.

'I'm sorry,' Sherman said. 'I would never have deliberately hurt you.'

She looked up at him with her dark eyes. 'It was not you,' she replied.

Kittredge felt awkward. 'What will you do now?' he asked.

The woman moved to her horse. 'I think I come with you,' she said.

Kittredge and Sherman were hesitant. This was a situation they had certainly never looked for.

'We have business,' Kittredge said. 'Perhaps there is somewhere we could take you?'

'I come with you,' she repeated.

Kittredge didn't know what to say. He looked to Sherman but he was equally at a loss.

'OK,' Kittredge said. He paused for a moment, wondering what else to say.

'Guess we'd better introduce ourselves,' he said then. 'My name's Kittredge, Dean Kittredge, and this here is Tad Sherman.'

They both held out their hands in an embarrassed way.

'I am Carmelita,' she said.

CHAPTER FIVE

They hadn't been riding for long when Carmelita moved her pinto alongside Sherman's buckskin.

'You know you are being followed?' she asked.

Sherman raised himself in his stirrups.

'You won't see them. They know how to conceal themselves,' she told him.

Kittredge turned to Sherman. 'We weren't wrong about that dust plume,' he said.

'They are Comancheros belonging to Gonsalez but they ride with others,' Carmelita said.

Kittredge turned to her. 'Gonsalez!' he said. 'What do you know about Gonsalez?'

She spat into the sand. 'Only that he is a poisonous snake. He is well named "El Serpiente". He is a snake and a bad man.'

Sherman and Kittredge exchanged looks, enlightenment dawning on them both.

'Is that where you got those bruises?' Sherman asked.

She did not reply but instead glared at them both, then spat again. Kittredge was thinking hard.

'You know where Gonsalez is to be found?'

Again Carmelita remained silent. Kittredge was aware that he was dealing with an unpredictable woman and a situation about which he knew next to nothing. He didn't know just how the woman felt about the bandit chief. Her dislike was obvious, but did that mean she would be willing to help them?

'Is Gonsalez at the Spanish Bit?'

She looked closely at Kittredge but he could not read any meaning into her expression. He decided that it might be better to say nothing further on the subject, at least not for the moment. He looked about him. The air shimmered and it was hard to judge distances. Far off things seemed near at hand and strangely distorted. A remote mesa might be closer than it looked. It was Carmelita who broke the awkward silence.

'Those men come for you. I think you need to deal with them.'

Kittredge turned to Sherman. 'She's got a point,' he said. 'I don't know about you, but I'm gettin' a mite nervous with those gunnies on our trail.'

'Reckon we're gonna have to deal with 'em sooner or later,' Sherman replied.

The woman pointed in another direction. 'There is somebody else,' she said. 'Not Comancheros.'

'How do you know? I can't see anythin'.'

'I know.'

Kittredge's eyes scanned the desert. There was nothing he could see but emptiness relieved only by some contorted rock formations and, further away, the mesa. A solitary buzzard flew through the blue air. A thought came to him.

'If we could follow those Comancheros,' he said, 'they might lead us to Gonsalez.'

Carmelita looked at him, then suddenly shook her head. 'They come for you to kill you. They will not go to Gonsalez.'

'Not sure I like the sound of that,' Kittredge said.

'I will show you where to find Gonsalez,' Carmelita said.

Kittredge tried not to show his surprise.

'I will show you where to find El Serpiente,' she repeated. 'But first we deal with gunmen.'

Kittredge took note of the inclusive meaning in her words. He wasn't sure about how to deal with her but he was quickly becoming convinced of her hatred for Gonsalez, a hatred that seemed to extend to his men. It wasn't hard to figure how it might have been between Carmelita and El Serpiente.

'Look!' she said.

Kittredge and Sherman both looked in the direction she indicated. A smudge of dust had appeared and even as they watched it seemed to come closer.

'They are here,' she said. 'It is not time to talk. Follow me.' Without waiting she turned and started riding hard.

'Guess she's taken control,' Kittredge joked.

He and Sherman spurred their horses and started after her. For a short time the three of them continued to ride at some pace, but then she brought her horse to an easy jog. She was a good rider. They carried on in this fashion for a little longer, nobody speaking, till they reached a thicket of brush and mesquite where Carmelita drew to a halt.

'This will do,' she said. She slid from the saddle and dragged her horse to the ground. 'You too,' she said.

She drew a piece of cloth from her saddle-bags and proceeded to blindfold her horse. Kittredge had expected her to make for the rocks, but he didn't wait to argue with her about it. Instead he and Sherman followed her example, after which they all covered the horses with brush, calming them with whispered words as they did so. They took their rifles and lay down in the brush nearby, as near to being undetectable as the barren landscape would allow.

'Now we wait,' Carmelita said when they had the horses quiet.

'How do you know they will pass this way?' Kittredge asked.

By way of reply she produced a glass bead and pointed it towards the sun. 'They will see the flash,' she said, 'and think it comes from your harness.'

They settled down to wait. While they did so Kittredge began to have his doubts. Was this woman leading them into some kind of trap? What did they know about her? He looked sideways at her. Her face was a mask. One thing was for certain, and that was that she had no fear of the gunnies they were waiting for. He wondered whether she was as good with a rifle as she was with a horse. He looked closely at her weapon. It was a carbine, the sort suited to cavalry use. He checked his own rifle and sidearms.

Sweat was rolling down his back and swarms of flies

hovered over the brush in which they were lying. A spider walked across his hand and he found himself worrying about snakes. This kind of cover would be ideal for a diamondback.

His thoughts reverted to the woman. Why had she jumped Sherman and almost killed him? He glanced towards Sherman. He lay with his rifle cradled against his uninjured shoulder. His wound did not appear to be troubling him. He had the woman who had caused it to thank for attending to it and binding it up. She was a mass of contradictions.

'Why did you stay with us?' Kittredge asked. 'You could have been long gone by now.'

She looked across at him. 'You are enemy of Gonsalez,' she replied.

Kittredge was thirsty and was just reaching for his canteen when Sherman's voice rose into the air:

'Here they come!'

They watched as the dust cloud grew bigger. Through the haze Kittredge could make out a number of riders. They came on at a steady pace, which surprised him for a moment till he remembered that they were well concealed. Closer and closer they rode till Kittredge could clearly see that there were eight of them. He glanced at the others. Their rifles were raised and they were deep in concentration. He turned back just as the riders suddenly came to a halt.

'What's happenin'?' he whispered.

'They are suspicious,' Carmelita replied. 'They are Comancheros. They know the land. They are not stupid.'

Kittredge calculated the distance between them. They were just out of range. One of them got down from his horse and began to inspect the ground.

'They know we are somewhere near,' Carmelita said.

Kittredge nodded. After all, the whole idea had been to draw them into a trap. The man rose from his haunches and began pointing back the way the three of them had ridden. He got back on his horse and took up a conversation with one of the other riders. All of them drew their rifles. Then they began to spread out.

'I don't like this,' Kittredge mumbled, more to himself than anyone else.

He had been hoping they would continue to come on in a bunch. This way they made themselves a harder target. The riders began to circle as they moved closer.

'You take the ones on the right,' Kittredge hissed to Sherman. 'Carmelita, you take the middle. I'll take the left. Fire when I give the signal.'

For a few more moments there was silence, broken only by the buzz of flies, then all hell seemed to break loose as a deafening volley of shots rang out and bullets pinged through the still desert air. Smoke billowed from the muzzles of the gunnies' rifles as they began a rapid continuous burst of firing. Still Kittredge waited, his ears deafened by the noise.

'OK!' he shouted. 'Let them have it!'

Taking careful aim, he squeezed the trigger of his Winchester. The rifle kicked, spitting flame and lead, and at the same instant there was a burst of fire from his companions. When the smoke cleared he could see two horses lying on the ground. He took aim once more;

there was a rapid fusillade of shots and he realized that there was no longer the luxury of picking a target.

His gun clicked on an empty chamber and as quickly as he could he jammed in fresh cartridges and began firing again. Carmelita and Sherman were pumping bullets in a steady stream but the blanket of gunsmoke hung so thick that it was impossible to tell what effect they were having. Shots were slicing into the brush all round them and the situation was getting decidedly uncomfortable.

Suddenly Kittredge tensed. He could smell burning and, turning his head, he saw more smoke billowing from the brush behind him. Tongues of flame burst like desert flowers and he realized with a sinking heart that the Comancheros had set fire to the brush. The blind-folded horses had lain still but now, sensing the presence of fire, they started to whinny and shift their legs, struggling to rise.

Just then the smoke in front of him dispersed suffi-ciently for Kittredge to see more of what was happening and his heart sank even lower. There were bodies of men and horses lying in the sand but the number of Comancheros seemed not to have dwindled. In fact there seemed to be more of them and he could only surmise that the eight riders they had seen were just the forerunners of a larger party. He turned to the others and tried making his voice heard above the staccato rattle of gunfire.

'It's no use! We're gonna have to make a break!'

Whether his words were heard by the others or not was a question that was destined to go unanswered, because just at that moment the whole desert around them seemed to erupt as though a volcano had blown its top. Dirt and debris flew into the sky and came rattling down on top of them. Kittredge's ears were deafened by the huge explosion and a blinding flash of light seared his eyes like a furnace. A wall of air hit him, leaving him momentarily stunned. When he had gathered his senses sufficiently he looked to see what had happened to the others and was relieved to see that they both seemed OK. But the fire behind them had spread and they were in danger of being surrounded by the flames.

'What the hell was that?' Sherman shouted.

Carmelita looked from one to the other of them, equally apprehensive. Kittredge became aware that the cacophony of gunfire had ceased. Wiping the dust from his eyes, he attempted to peer out. A heap of horses and men lay in grotesque attitudes in the sand and near by the ground had opened up to form a smoking crater. Riding away into the distance were the surviving Comancheros.

'I don't know what happened,' Kittredge said. 'But let's get out of here.'

With the fire getting perilously close, they removed the blindfolds from the horses and, trying to keep them calm, led them into the open, where they mounted.

'Head for those rocks!' Kittredge shouted.

The rocks were in the opposite direction to that from which the Comancheros had come and Kittredge reasoned that if there was another attack the cover provided by the rocks would be their best bet. It wasn't far. As they rode he looked back over his shoulder but there was no sign of pursuit. A great column of smoke still hung in the air but the fire seemed to be dying out. He still couldn't work out what had happened.

The main pinnacle of rock towered over them as they rode through a gap between some large boulders and entered a kind of cleft. They continued a little further, then suddenly Sherman, who was riding in front, drew to a halt. The others pulled up behind him.

'What the hell!' Sherman began.

Standing in front of them was a covered wagon, the canvas of which had been drawn back. Inside was what appeared to be some huge machine, a sinister-looking monster that seemed to threaten them with its open mouth. Kittredge's jaw dropped in surprise when, as if that wasn't enough, round the corner of the wagon emerged none other than the old quack, Grattan, grinning at them with his snaggle-toothed mouth.

'Saw you ridin' this way,' he said. 'Surprised you didn't come right on in when I seen those Comancheros comin' after you.'

Kittredge was too amazed to say anything. It was Sherman who recovered his composure first.

'Grattan!' he said. 'What in hell are you doin' here? And just what is that inside your wagon?'

The oldster spat into the dirt.

'Guess it must seem kinda strange. Let me introduce you to ol' Thunder. Don't get to see much of her since the war ended.'

He jumped up on to the wagon and pulled the canvas a little further apart. Kittredge got down from

98

his horse and approached the wagon. Now he could see what the strange instrument was.

'A Williams gun!' he exclaimed. 'So that's what caused the explosion!'

'Yup sirree,' the oldster said. 'First time she's been fired in anger since Seven Pines.'

Sherman and Carmelita came up alongside the wagon.

'She's past the limit of her range,' Grattan said. 'I only figured to kinda scare those *hombres* off. Guess it was just a lucky strike.'

'What is Williams gun?' Carmelita said.

'Confederate cannon,' Kittredge replied.

Carmelita's look was uncomprehending.

'Guess it weren't any of your concern. Besides, I s'pose you'd be kinda young to remember,' Kittredge said. 'How come you have it, old fella?'

'Call it one of the spoils of war. Never figured to fire it again in anger. Sure felt good to let the old girl have her say.'

'You used one of these things before?'

'Sure. Normally took three men, but I can manage. Used to be an engineer. Made some modifications.' He was suddenly reflective.

'Hell, I might not look like much now, but I used to cut a mighty dashin' figure. Rode with the Kentucky Cavalry.' He paused. 'Maybe I shouldn't be tellin' you fellas this,' he said.

Kittredge grunted. 'War's been over a long time,' he said. 'We're all friends again now.'

'Where do you keep it?' Sherman asked, scratching

his stubbly beard in astonishment.

'Bits of her here, bits of her there. Lucky for you she was pretty well assembled when I saw what was goin' on with you and those gunnies.'

'But what are you doin' here?' Kittredge repeated. 'Last time I saw you, you were headin' for Arrowhead.'

'Yeah. Let's say Arrowhead weren't just as right friendly as I figured it'd be. Bought me a few stores while I was there and decided to hit the trail again. Normally I'd be tradin' with those Comancheros but I got reason to suspect those days could be over.'

'Why?' Sherman said. 'You been comin' and goin' between here and Arrowhead for a long time.'

'Things has changed since that coyote Gonsalez took over. Folks call him "El Serpiente". It's sure been quick and downright poisonous the way things have gone since he took control.' Grattan looked at Carmelita. 'Say, ain't you his woman? Sorry if I've said anythin' to upset you.'

Carmelita's face twisted into a scowl. 'Gonsalez is a gila monster,' she said. 'He is vermin. I will not rest till he is crushed.'

Grattan looked at the bruises on her face. 'Guess you got your own reasons,' he replied.

'We all got reasons to dislike Gonsalez,' Kittredge said. 'Question is, what do we do now?'

'Whatever you decide,' Grattan said, 'count me in.'

Carmelita was looking closely at the gun. 'Can this be moved?' she said.

Grattan nodded. 'Sure. She's been hidden here for a long while, at least a good part of her, and she might be a bit sanded-up and rusty, but I figure we could manage.'

Kittredge turned to the woman. 'What are you thinkin'?' he asked.

'I know where Gonsalez is to be found. I have said I will take you there but the way is not easy.'

'That mesa,' Grattan said. 'My guess is that he's hidden away somewhere up there.'

Carmelita grinned. She had good teeth but Kittredge noticed for the first time that some of them had been broken.

'You are clever,' she said. 'Maybe it's you who should be named "El Serpiente".'

'I figured it out,' he replied.

'You are right, but the mesa is a very strange and secret place. There are many canyons and hidden trails. It is a maze where a man might get lost and not find his way out.'

Grattan looked at Kittredge and Sherman. 'Well?' he said. 'What do you reckon?'

'I reckon we go into that serpent's nest and roust him out,' Kittredge said.

Grattan looked at the gun. 'If you're figurin' to move that old critter, it's gonna need all your strength once we get to the mesa,' he said. 'I ain't hauled it through no mountains before.'

'You are strong men,' Carmelita replied. 'And you have already declared war on the Comancheros.'

Kittredge looked back at the sight of the recent battle. A flock of buzzards hung over the scene.

'How many men does Gonsalez have at his

command?' he asked.

Carmelita shrugged. 'They are many, perhaps fifty, perhaps a hundred. But they are never all there at the same time.'

Kittredge was a little dubious about the numbers. Whatever talents Carmelita might possess, arithmetic did not appear to be one of them.

'Long odds,' he said.

'You got the gun,' she replied.

'If we can ever get it as far as that mesa.'

'Like I say,' Grattan interjected, 'that will be the easy part.'

Back at the Scissors Crudace was surprised one morning to see Brigstock riding into the yard. He was the second visitor he had received in as many days, the other being Marshal Stegner. The marshal had asked him some awkward questions regarding what had taken place at the Rafter W and, while he had no reason to suppose that Stegner suspected him in any way, it was still with a slight sense of nervousness that he stepped on to the veranda to greet the Rafter W man.

'Hello,' he said. 'You seem to be a bit out of your way?'

'I got somethin' for you,' Brigstock replied.

Without getting down from his horse he felt in an inside pocket. After a moment's fumbling he came up with an envelope, which he handed over to Crudace.

'It's from Miss Waggoner,' he said.

Crudace felt annoyed but did not show it. 'Is she expectin' a reply?' he asked.

'She didn't say so.' Brigstock tugged at the reins of his horse.

'Won't you stay for a drink?' Crudace said.

Brigstock shook his head. 'Reckon I'd better be gettin' back,' he replied.

Crudace gave a kind of shrug. The next moment Brigstock had ridden off and Crudace went back inside the ranch house.

He sat down at a desk, opened a drawer and produced a bottle of bourbon, from which he poured himself a stiff drink. He tore open the envelope. Inside was a single sheet of paper, which he unfolded and proceeded to read:

I do not have time to elaborate. Meet me in Arrowhead at noon tomorrow. The usual place.

It was brief and to the point and this only added to the irritation he was beginning to feel. It seemed to him that Miss Trashy had no call to adopt this peremptory tone. Who was she, after all? He had been tiring of her for some time and he almost regretted having got involved with her in the first place. Still, she had been useful to him in the past and maybe there was something in this that might be to his advantage. But it was still irritating. He had other concerns on his mind at the moment to do with Gonsalez and his crew of deadbeats which might mean his having to pay a visit to the Spanish Bit. Maybe getting involved with Gonsalez was another thing to regret. What was that ridiculous name Gonsalez liked to be known by? El Serpiente? Well, first

103

he would see what Miss Trashy wanted. He could deal with Gonsalez easy enough.

It was not long after dawn when Carmelita mounted her horse and led her new-found companions out of the shadows of the rock pinnacle in the direction of the distant mesa. There was a bracing chill to the air but it would not be long after the sun gathered its strength. Alongside her rode Sherman and Kittredge with the old-timer Grattan bringing up the rear in his wagon. Nothing was said. Kittredge scanned the desert as they rode, checking for any signs of the Comancheros who had attacked them the day before, but there had been no disturbances during the night and they were probably quite far away.

Ahead of them the mesa was a dark smudge in the distance. As the day progressed it changed colour, becoming dark purple, then red. As the sun strengthened and the heat grew, the air began to shimmer and the mesa seemed insubstantial, almost appearing to float in the air just above the desert floor.

Kittredge began to question whether it might not have been more sensible to journey by night, but Carmelita seemed oblivious of the heat and discomfort. She wore a wide sombrero and Kittredge found himself envying her the shade it offered. Towards mid-morning she lifted it from her head and pointed towards a slight depression in the ground. When they rode down it they found a trickle of water and a brackish pool among the rocks. They dismounted and let the horses and the mules take a drink.

'You know the country,' Kittredge said. 'We would have missed it.'

'*Sí*, I know the land. To the gringo it is harsh and cruel, but it is not so to someone who respects it.'

Kittredge looked towards the mesa. It did not seem to be any closer than when they had set out. They ate some pemmican, then climbed back into leather. They carried on, travelling at a slow pace in order to accommodate the wagon with its heavy load, moving like ants across the rusty scarred landscape. Dust hung thick about them and a hot wind arose, blowing into their faces. Kittredge and Sherman pulled down the brims of their Stetsons and pulled up their bandannas as a means of protection. Plumes of dust ran across the desert and hovered in the air. Clouds of flies accompanied them. Kittredge's head began to ache and his throat grew parched. He looked up and the mesa seemed still no nearer.

As they struggled on he became aware of another sound above the buzz of the flies and the soughing of the wind. It had been going on for some time before he registered it. It was someone singing. Almost doubting the evidence of his ears, Kittredge looked back at the wagon, to see Grattan sitting high on the box and exercising his lungs with a version of what Kittredge recognized, after a few more moments of listening, as The Bonnie Blue Flag. He couldn't help but grin. The oldster didn't seem to mind the discomforts of travel one bit. He was as happy and as at home as if he had been sitting on his own front porch.

Then Kittredge thought about what the oldster had

said about fighting with the Kentucky cavalry. Hadn't the old buzzard told him the first time they met that he had been invalided out of the struggle after the first Bull Run? Whichever was true, the oldster certainly had something of a limp, which made it all the more remarkable that he had coped with the Williams gun. It would be an idea to check out that old cannon again before they got as far as the mesa. A time might come when they would need it to be in good working order.

Crudace was at the window of his office, looking out for Miss Trashy. He glanced at the clock, whose ticking was the only sound to be heard apart from occasional muffled sounds of people passing in the street. It was typical of her to be late. He felt annoyed. Then he saw her turning the corner below. Quickly she glanced right and left and then disappeared from sight. In a moment he heard her footsteps on the stairs. He opened his door just as she reached the landing, panting slightly from the exertion. He had to admit that she looked beautiful.

'You took care nobody saw you enter?' he questioned.

'Of course. Do you need to ask?'

'What about that dolt Brigstock? He brought me your letter. Doesn't he suspect anything? Surely he must?'

She shrugged her shoulders in a careless gesture.

'Who cares if he does?' she said. She looked at him coyly.

'Mr Crudace, you haven't even kissed me yet. Aren't

106

you pleased to see me?'

Crudace looked up to make sure the door was closed, then took her in his arms.

'There, that's better,' she said. 'I was beginning to wonder if you hadn't grown tired of your little old pussy cat.'

She sat down, removing her gloves, while he poured a couple of drinks.

'Naughty man,' she said. 'I do believe that is alcohol you are offering me. What if Brigstock smells it on my breath?'

Crudace sat down beside her. He was beginning to be irritated by her conversation. How had it ever appealed to him in the first place?

'About that letter,' he said. 'It sounded rather mysterious. What was it you didn't have time to elaborate on?'

She threw her head back and laughed. Crudace felt the old stab of desire at the sight of her neck and throat.

'You are in a hurry today,' she said. 'Let me take some time to relax. It's a tiresome journey from the Rafter W.'

Crudace got up and took a cheroot from a case. He clipped the end.

'You don't mind?' he said.

'No, of course not. In fact, I like it when you smoke. It makes you seem – I don't know – more manly.'

He lit the cheroot and inhaled the smoke, taking his time to enjoy it. He was beginning to suspect that there was no real significance to the note. It was probably just another of Miss Trashy's tricks. She liked to feel important.

'Well?' he said.

'Well what?'

'About the note?'

'Oh, you are being rather insistent.' She paused, giving him an upward glance.

'All right,' she said. 'First of all, I thought it might be of some interest to you to know that Kittredge and that old fool Sherman have been absent from the Rafter W. At first I didn't notice, but when I did I started asking around. Nobody seemed to know anything. In the end I got it from my grandfather. He always lets things kind of slip when I apply a little subtle pressure. Isn't the Spanish Bit one of your properties?'

Crudace was interested now. 'Yes, it is. What of it?'

'Well, it seems that Kittredge and Sherman are heading in that direction.'

She looked at Crudace and couldn't help but observe the intent look on his swarthy features.

'Are you pleased with your little kitten now?' she said.

Crudace regarded her with an absent look in his eyes before snapping back to attention.

'Of course, my pretty,' he replied.

'Something else has been worrying me,' she said. 'Some of Grandfather's cattle were found shot and killed. Please tell me that wasn't you?'

Crudace wasn't sure what she was referring to but set about placating her. 'Cattle killed? How can you suggest—'

'Oh, please don't take it amiss. I only thought . . . you know, the night of the dance, when I told you most of the men would be in town.'

'Is that when it happened? It must have been some of those Comancheros who've been seen around.'

He sat down next to her and she leaned on his shoulder. 'I'm so sorry,' he whispered. 'It must have been very upsetting, for you and your grandfather. If there's anything I can do. . . .'

His words petered out. The scent of Miss Trashy's hair was intoxicating and her breasts were heaving as she sobbed gently.

'It's all right,' he said. 'Big cross old cinnamon bear has been unkind to his little kitty.' He raised her head and kissed her on the lips. Her eyes were damp and shining.

'Big old bear will have to make up to his kitty-cat,' he murmured.

Over Miss Trashy's shoulders he glanced at the clock.

After two days of hard travelling, Carmelita, Kittredge, Sherman and Grattan were at last approaching the mesa. On the second night they had set up camp almost in its shadow and, as the morning sun rose in the sky, Kittredge observed it closely through his field glasses. The walls towered more than 1,000 feet into the air, and were split and cracked with entrances to canyons. The mesa top glowed red with the sunrise, the rimrock projecting over the pitted and eroded cliff walls like battlements. Kittredge reckoned the entire mesa to be about five miles long and three miles wide, and they were approaching its narrower side. He lowered the glasses as approaching footsteps heralded the arrival of Carmelita.

'It is grand, is it not?' she said. 'A man could hide out there for a long time. It is a world of its own.' She bent down and began to scrabble in the sand, digging something from the ground.

'Look,' she said. 'Men have lived here long before us.' She handed the object to Kittredge. It was a broken piece of pottery.

'There is no need to look far,' she said. 'I have also found stone tools.'

Kittredge looked around. 'You are right,' he said. 'There must have been Indian people living here long ago, settled people, not travellers like the Navajo.'

'You will see,' she said. 'There are houses built high up in the cliffs. They are hidden where no one would go. El Serpiente uses one cliff village as his headquarters.'

Kittredge glanced behind him. 'Will we be able to get the wagon through?' he asked.

Carmelita shrugged. 'We can only try,' she said.

When they were ready they rolled out of camp. The mesa was like a giant sphinx lying across the land, slightly higher at one end than the other. Kittredge for one felt threatened by its huge bulk. As they got close they could see that they were heading for a deep canyon that only now became clearly visible. It was wide and there was plenty of room for the wagon to go through. Once they were inside the mesa the canyon opened out further so that it was eventually more like a deep valley.

The morning sun glanced from the bluish rock and high up on the mountain sides they caught the glint of

110

water. By contrast with the stifling heat of the desert, the valley was cool and the air refreshing. The mesa was, as Carmelita had said, a world of its own. As they moved further into the plateau they crossed a narrow runnel of water which became a thin stream and, when the trail took a turn, Kittredge spotted movement on the opposite bank further ahead.

'Cattle!' he exclaimed.

'Gonsalez keeps some of the cows he steal,' Carmelita said. 'Some of them escape and find their way through the mountain passes.'

Sherman turned to her. 'You will show us where Gonsalez keeps his cattle hidden?'

'*Sí*, I will show you. It is a secret place. Gonsalez's men know of it but it would remain hidden from the outsider.'

Sherman turned his horse and splashed through the shallow water. There were three cows standing together; when he reached them he jumped down from the saddle and looked closely to see if there were any markings. Two of them he didn't recognize but there was no mistaking the third. He climbed back in the saddle and rode back to the others.

'Rafter W,' he said. 'Looks like we were right about those missin' cows.'

Carmelita looked at him. 'They are your cows?' she said.

Sherman nodded. 'We figured some of 'em might have been hazed down as far as the Spanish Bit.'

'There's probably some of 'em at the Spanish Bit as well as here,' Kittredge remarked. 'But the fact that

111

they are here at all means El Serpiente has been double-dealin' our friend Crudace. I wonder whether he knows anythin' about this?' He turned to Carmelita. 'Have you heard of a man called Crudace?'

Carmelita's brows contracted in thought. 'I think I hear El Serpiente mention the name,' she said. 'I think Gonsalez no like this man Crudace.'

Kittredge grinned. 'There'd be no surprise in that,' he said.

Grattan had been listening to the exchange. 'I know this Crudace,' he said. 'Ain't he the joker with the office in Arrowhead? Seen him about from time to time. You figure he's involved with Gonsalez?'

'Ain't got no proof could hold up in a court of law,' Kittredge replied. 'But there's little doubt there's a connection.'

'Find any of those cow critters on the Spanish Bit, I figure you got proof enough.'

They started to move on. The sun was sufficiently high now to flood the valley with its rays, although part of the eastern wall remained in shadow. The rock walls began to close in again and the path got more rugged, becoming quite steep in places. Ahead of them the trail seemed to end in a solid wall of rock, but when they had gone another half mile or so they saw a further opening in the cliffs to their right. Carmelita indicated that they were to turn off and head towards it.

The entrance here was narrower than the passage into the mesa and the trail ascended at a sharper angle. Grattan was having problems with the wagon. Despite his best efforts, the mules were finding the strain too much and the wheels were sinking into the soft earth. Kittredge and Sherman dismounted and climbed into the back of the wagon to see if something could be done about lessening and redistributing the weight. There was a rough wooden box in one corner and when Kittredge made to move it he found it was a lot heavier than he had imagined.

'Grattan!' he shouted. 'What you got in this crate?'

In a moment the oldster's face appeared through the canvas with a big grin.

'I meant to tell you about those old things,' he said. 'Go ahead, open the lid and take a look.'

Kittredge did as he suggested, then staggered back with a horrified expression on his countenance,

'Grenades!' he gasped. 'This rig could blow to high hell!'

Grattan chuckled. 'No fear of that,' he said. 'They're harmless till the fuse has been lit.'

Kittredge and Sherman didn't look too convinced as they both leaped down from the wagon.

'They're Union grenades, ain't they? Hell, which side were you on?' asked Kettredge.

'They might look like Union grenades but they ain't. Those fellas are Rains grenades. Look a bit like a Ketchum but the head is different and they got a streamer.'

'Where did you pick these up?' Sherman asked.

'Same place I got the gun.'

Kittredge got back up to take a further look.

'Figure they could come in mighty useful too,' Grattan said.

'Yeah?' Kittredge replied. 'More likely if we throw 'em anywhere near Gonsalez he'll pick 'em up and throw 'em straight back again.'

'Either that or they'll blow our hands off before we ever get to chuck 'em,' Sherman added.

Grattan laughed. 'You show a distinct lack of faith,' he said. 'The old gun didn't let us down, did it?'

Kittredge exchanged glances with the others. 'Let's get this wagon movin',' he said.

Gingerly they lifted down the box of grenades together with various other items. It didn't seem to make much difference and Sherman contemplated lifting down the gun. It wasn't something he relished doing and once again he wondered at Grattan's ability to perform the unexpected. How had he manoeuvred the gun into position? It was a wonder the old wagon had ever survived the shock of the detonation.

They didn't need to lift down the gun, however, because when Grattan cracked his whip the wagon lumbered forward with a lurch. It was still hard going but after a short time the gradient levelled out and they were able to move forward without too much difficulty along the floor of the canyon. Kittredge, Sherman and Carmelita walked alongside the wagon. Shadows were already descending from the high rock walls. It seemed to Kittredge that they had entered another world, a strange and secret world where the outside rules no longer applied. In this world even Grattan's behaviour seemed almost normal and anything might happen.

CHAPTER SIX

It was late when Crudace and his assorted crew of cowhands and roughnecks rode into the yard of the Spanish Bit. Since his incarnation as land agent and rancher, Crudace had grown soft. The easy life had bitten into his bones and he was less than happy after the hard ride and the exigencies of the desert. He had sent word on ahead that he was coming, and he expected everything to have been arranged for his comfort when he arrived. The fact that nothing was prepared and his arrival was quite unexpected put him in an even worse frame of mind. While his men made their way to the bunkhouse he stormed through the ranch house door.

'Crombie!' he yelled. 'Where the hell is everybody?'

He stamped his way through to the kitchen and then called up the stairs. 'Crombie!'

He waited for a few moments but there was no answering call. There was no sign of his foreman or of anybody else. Furiously, he threw open the door of a cabinet and produced a bottle of brandy. He poured himself a stiff drink, then sank back into the enveloping comfort of an armchair. A short time passed, then there was a knock on the door.

'Come in!' Crudace yelled.

The door opened and a worried-faced Crombie appeared. Crudace looked him up and down.

'What the hell is going on?' he snapped. 'I sent Rogers down to let you know I was headed this way. What sort of welcome is this?'

'Sorry, boss,' Crombie muttered. 'Somethin' must have happened to Rogers on the way here. We ain't seen hide nor hair of him.'

Crudace tossed back the remainder of his drink and then poured another.

'Never mind that now,' he said. 'Just round up the cook and get him to rustle up a meal. Somethin' decent. I ain't eaten properly in days.'

There were noises from the direction of the bunkhouse.

'The boys seem to makin' themselves at home,' Crudace remarked. He broke off to light a cheroot which he had taken from a box on a table. 'How have things been down here?' he barked.

'Quiet,' Crombie replied. 'Things is just tickin' along. We got a few new head of steers some of Gonsalez's men drove in.' He was surprised at the look of hatred which spread across Crudace's features.

'I'd be willin' to bet there's a good few missin',' the rancher said. 'I'll be takin' a look around first thing in the mornin'. After that make sure the boys are ready because I want to talk to 'em and you can be sure I

116

won't be mincin' my words.'

Crombie struggled with himself for a moment before asking:

'Is there a problem, boss?'

'Too right,' Crudace snarled. 'And I'll give you one guess as to who I'm referrin' to.'

Crosbie thought for only a second. 'Gonsalez?' he hazarded.

'You got it in one. I figure it's time Gonsalez was taught a lesson.'

Crombie wasn't too sure what his boss was referring to but made a quick decision to say nothing. He didn't have to wait long for things to be made clearer.

'That no-good cheatin' son of a coyote has been holdin' back on me for too long. How many cows do you figure he's stolen from the Spanish Bit all this time? I figure he's holdin' more head of cattle than we are.'

Crombie didn't like to comment that since the cattle had either been stolen in the first place or were the outcome of Gonsalez's dealings with the Comanche, Crudace had little cause to complain on that score.

'That stinkin' polecat owes me money and just lately he's been gettin' way too big for his boots,' Crudace continued. 'It's time he was cut down to size and that's just what I intend doin'. El Serpiente is sure gonna get one hell of a shock next time he decides to put in an appearance at the Spanish Bit.'

Crudace's expression had changed as if the mere prospect of dealing with Gonsalez in his own way was a source of satisfaction. He addressed Crombie in a less hostile manner.

117

'Go on, then. Roust out that good for nothin' cook, whatever he's doin', and let's start gettin' this show on the road.'

Feeling somewhat relieved, his foreman moved out of the room, shutting the door quietly behind him.

Kittredge was becoming a little confused. Led by Carmelita, their little party had advanced deep into the mesa, following a route that led through a maze of canyons and winding trails. Now, as they slowly advanced down one more path overhung by high rock walls, she suddenly held up her hand as a signal for them to halt.

'What is it?' asked Kittredge.

'You want to see where El Serpiente keeps the stolen cattle?' she replied.

'Sure,' Kittredge answered. He turned to Sherman. 'Figure that would be real useful to know, don't you?' he said.

'Sure do. Most of those critters are probably ours.'

Grattan took a bite from a wad of tobacco. 'You boys go on ahead,' he said. 'Me and the mules will wait here and take a break.'

Kittredge nodded. 'OK,' he said to Carmelita. 'Where do we go from here?'

'Follow me,' she said. 'But when we get closer we must take care. Some of Gonsalez's men might be on duty up there.'

Kittredge had been wondering when they might make some sort of contact with the enemy. He had expected that there might be guards at various points, but so far there had been no mention of the Comancheros and certainly no sighting of them. At times Kittredge had felt that they were vulnerable but he could see why Gonsalez would not bother to set a watch over the way they had come so far. The passage into the mesa was so tortuous and complicated that he would have deemed it unnecessary.

'What about the horses?' he asked.

'There is no problem yet with the horses,' she replied. 'When we get closer we dismount and make the last part on foot.'

She set off up the trail, Kittredge and Sherman following in single file. They hadn't gone far when she turned off down a narrow cleft which any other rider would probably have missed and which began to open out as the surrounding rock walls fell away and the path ascended. At length they came to a growth of trees where she ordered them to dismount.

'We leave the horses here,' she said. 'There is not much further to go and they will be concealed.'

After securing the horses they moved forward on foot through the trees. The way led upward and as the trees thinned out Kittredge could see that they were approaching a summit. Panting slightly from the exertion, they emerged on to the brow of the hill.

'Keep low!' Carmelita hissed.

Suiting action to her words, she dropped to the ground. Kittredge and Sherman followed suit. Crawling forward a little further, they arrived at a position from which they had a good view of the scene below them. It was a narrow valley, hemmed in by hills and high rock

119

walls and even from a distance Kittredge could see that the valley floor was covered with a thick growth of grass. The place was like an oasis, the temperature and conditions mild and temperate because of its high location in the heart of the mesa. Scattered all about the valley were groups of cattle, leisurely cropping the herbage. A narrow stream ran through one side of the valley, providing a more than adequate source of water. For the first time, Kittredge could see signs of human activity. Towards the far side of the valley were some huts and a corral with horses.

'It's a nice set-up Gonsalez has here,' Sherman remarked.

'*Sí*, he has it all, but I will take it from him.'

Kittredge glanced sideways at Carmelita. Her face was taut with hatred and he wondered what else Gonsalez had done to incur her wrath. She turned to face Sherman and her look softened.

'Together, we destroy El Serpiente,' she said.

Sherman grinned somewhat uncomfortably. 'Sure,' he said.

Kittredge felt a need to intervene. 'We only got about fifty of his Comancheros to deal with first,' he commented. 'Isn't that what you said?'

Carmelita shrugged. 'Fifty, one hundred. What does it matter? We have the big gun.'

Kittredge did not share her faith. As far as he was concerned, both the gun and the grenades were likely to prove more of a liability than anything.

'Is this where Gonsalez is based?' Kittredge said.

'No, *señor*. Some of his men live here but El

Serpiente is more cunning. He has his own place which I show you next.'

'OK,' Kittredge said, 'but right now maybe we'd better get back to Grattan.'

With one last glance at the valley below they slithered down from their vantage point and made their way back to the horses. Grattan was waiting just as they had left him, except that he had a fire going and strips of bacon sizzling in the pan.

'Figured we could do with some strengthenin',' he said.

'Sure appreciate it,' Kittredge replied. 'But aren't you takin' a risk? What if some of Gonsalez's men see the smoke?'

'They won't see any smoke,' he replied. 'I ain't no greenhorn.' He had built the fire in a sheltered spot beside an aspen tree and filled the coffee pot with water from a spring. By the time they had eaten and were on their second mug of coffee, Kittredge was feeling ready for action. He looked across the fire for Carmelita who was sitting close to Sherman. If circumstances had been different, he might have been tempted to think *too close*.

'How much further to Gonsalez's hideout?' he asked.

Carmelita said something in a low tone to Sherman, then turned her head towards Kittredge.

'It is not far now. Let me tell you how it is and you can decide what we must do.'

Kittredge nodded. 'Go ahead,' he said. 'What's the set-up?'

By way of reply she stood up. 'Come with me. I show you something.'

The three men got to their feet and followed her as she began walking down the path. A short way ahead the trail took a slight turn and when the others came alongside her she pointed at the sheer rock face high above them.

'See,' she said.

They looked. About three quarters of the way up the cliff stood some ruined buildings.

'What are they?' Sherman said.

'People built them long ago,' Carmelita replied. 'They have long been abandoned. It is in such a place, only bigger, that El Serpiente has his nest.'

Grattan spat a gob of tobacco juice. 'Hell,' he said. 'He must have wings to get up that high.'

Carmelita uttered a sound which was not quite a laugh. 'There is no need for wings,' she said. 'The place he has chosen has two ways in. There is a path, which few people know about, from the top of the mesa. It is not the only one. There is also a path from the floor of the canyon. The way is hard and narrow and in places there are steps. He has no fears of anyone finding their way to his hideout, so the place is but lightly guarded. Because of its situation, it should be possible for a small force such as we are to penetrate it by taking the trail up from the canyon.'

'This path?' Kittredge queried. 'We could get up it without too many problems?'

'Yes. I go first and lead the way.'

'OK,' Kittredge agreed. 'Seems to me that the best time to do this would be at night. We'd have a better chance of taking Gonsalez by surprise.'

122

Sherman nodded. 'Just what I was thinkin',' he remarked.

'It is good,' Carmelita said. 'I take you the rest of the way. It is not far. But from now on I think we take more care, leave horses and wagon behind.'

Grattan had remained silent, looking up at the mountainside and making some calculations. Now he spat once again before speaking.

'This place Gonsalez uses for his headquarters,' he said. 'Is it about the same height as this pueblo?'

'It is higher,' Carmelita replied.

Grattan considered her response. He looked back at the wagon.

'I ain't arguin' against what you bin sayin',' he said. 'But I ain't dragged that doggone gun all this way for nothin'. Tarnation, that just wouldn't be fair to those old mules. Now I bin lookin' up at that mountainside and those old ruins and considerin' whether a chance shot might be even more effective. Trouble is, I don't think the old girl would be that reliable and I figure the elevation would be just too great.'

'I'd almost forgotten that gun,' Kittredge said. 'You were lucky last time you fired it and I figure the next time it's more likely to blow up right in your own face than hit any target. But now you mention it, it does seem kind of a waste to bring it all this way for nothin'.'

'You could be right,' Grattan said. 'The way I look at it is this. Whichever way you approach this, there's gonna be shootin'. When that happens there'll be plenty more of those Comancheros appearing on the scene than show up at the start. You might need to get

123

away in a hurry.' He turned to Carmelita. 'Is the way we've come the only way in and out of the mesa?'

Carmelita shook her head. 'There's another route through from the side of the mesa. That's the way they usually drive in the cattle. There's also the route down from the top, but it's very difficult. Horses wouldn't be able to get down. Some of Gonsalez's men might head that way, but most of 'em will follow the trail we've just followed.'

Grattan considered her words carefully. 'Then here's what I propose. While you three go on ahead I'll stay behind near the last camp. From what Carmelita has said, those Comanchero varmints will come that way. I'll take the wagon back apiece to a position where I can set up the cannon.'

Kittredge thought about it. 'I'm not sure if it makes any sense,' he concluded, 'but I guess it's as good a plan as any. With that war injury of yours, you're never gonna make it up that path to the pueblo anyway. Let's get back now and set things up.'

'Sure could use a little help,' Grattan replied. 'And don't forget to take some of those grenades with you when you go. Should come in mighty useful.'

If Crudace had been in a bad mood when he arrived at the Spanish Bit, Miss Trashy, in her own way, was even more annoyed when she turned up at his office only to find him gone. After knocking furiously on the door she turned on her heel and made for Ma Kennedy's eating-house. She flounced in and ordered a coffee. Ma Kennedy observed her from the counter and easily guessed the source of her irritation. Ma Kennedy was no fool. She kept her ear to the ground and knew most of what was happening in Arrowhead. For once she derived some satisfaction from Miss Trashy's distress. She didn't like Crudace and she didn't like the way Miss Trashy had treated Sherman from the Rafter W.

Presently the door opened and, as Brigstock entered, Ma Kennedy discreetly disappeared behind the hangings leading to the kitchen.

'You took your time,' Miss Trashy said.

'Saw you through the window,' he replied. There had been no arrangement to meet her at this time but he didn't bother to pursue the matter.

'Everything all right, Miss Waggoner?' he said.

'No, everything is not all right.'

She felt an urge to let fly about Crudace but managed to hold her tongue. Did Brigstock know anything of her meetings with the land agent? Suddenly she felt reckless. She was tired of being ferried about by Brigstock or one of the other ranch hands. She was old enough to take care of herself.

'Come on,' she said. 'I want to go back to the ranch.'

'Sure, ma'am, anything you say.' He glanced at the half empty cup of coffee. 'Ain't you gonna finish your refreshments,' he said.

She did not reply but stormed out, leaving him to pay. When he got to the buggy she was perched in her seat and did not say anything further. As he mounted his horse she flicked the reins and the buggy took the road leading back to the Rafter W.

Miss Trashy barely noticed anything as they went

125

along. Her mind was whirling with emotions of anger, frustration and thwarted will. And the surprising thing was that as she bowled along the trail, it was Dean Kittredge she was thinking of, rather than anyone else.

Kittredge, Sherman and Carmelita crouched in the shadows of the rock wall below the cliff where Gonsalez had set up his headquarters in the old ruined pueblo. It was a clear night and the ribbon of sky overhead was thick with stars. The stone buildings of the pueblo seemed to glow with a faint ghostly radiance and along the ledge the dying remnants of a few fires still flickered. Whoever was up there seemed to have retired for the night.

'The path up to the ledge is here,' Carmelita whispered.

'Let's take a last check on our weapons,' Kittredge suggested.

In addition to their rifles and handguns, across Kittredge's shoulders and those of Sherman were slung bags containing some of the grenades, as many as they could comfortably carry. Carmelita had the carbine and her knife was strapped to her side.

'Remember, move silently,' she whispered.

Neither Kittredge nor Sherman could see anything resembling a break in the rock wall but they followed Carmelita as she made her way through some bushes to where a niche behind a boulder offered a tentative foothold. Agilely she clambered over some more rocks, Kittredge and Sherman following close behind. They emerged on a narrow cleft which led steeply upward. It

126

was hard going and before long Kittredge and Sherman were both panting for breath. Carmelita seemed not to feel the same discomfort and made headway at a quicker pace, having to stop every now and again for them to catch up. After a time they lost sight of the floor of the canyon as the track led into the mountain side.

As they climbed, they caught further glimpses of the ledge above them and the great cavern behind it. The little stone village seemed wrapped in an aura of time-lessness and mystery. Scuffling his way forward, Kittredge saw the figure of the woman standing upright a little way ahead. At this point the track levelled off and then fell away into nothingness. Across the gaping black void was stretched the trunk of a long-dead cedar tree.

'It is not so bad as it seems,' Carmelita said.

'It don't look too steady,' Sherman replied.

'How long's it been there?' asked Kittredge. 'Likely the whole thing will collapse as soon as somebody sets foot on it.'

'The fact that it has been there a long time is a good sign,' Carmelita said. 'Have no fear; I have been across it before.'

Kittredge looked dubious.

'Ain't no point worryin' about it,' Sherman said. 'Less'n we all want to go back again.'

'Just follow me and do what I do,' Carmelita said. She stepped on to the dried-out tree trunk and walked forward with no hesitation.

'Don't look down,' Kittredge advised, then he placed

his foot on to the trunk. It was quite wide and he followed Carmelita with a confident tread, opening his
arms wide like a tightrope walker. He heard a slight
sound behind him and it seemed that the tree trunk
moved slightly beneath his feet as Sherman stepped
forward.

Carmelita had already reached the other side and
stood making gestures of encouragement. Ignoring his
own advice to Sherman, Kittredge paused and glanced
down. There was nothing to see, just a pit of blackness,
but when he looked up and the stars swam into his
vision he experienced a sudden surge of panic. For a
moment he felt as if he were suspended in space. The
bag containing the grenades seemed suddenly to have
become very heavy and its weight badly distributed. He
closed his eyes, breathing deeply to try and calm his
growing sense of vertigo, then he stepped forward.

How he got to the end of the dizzy walkway he did
not know but all at once he felt the earth beneath his
feet and, taking another pace forward, he sank to the
ground. At the same moment Sherman came up.

'Are you OK?' Sherman whispered.

Kittredge nodded. 'Yup, I think so. But I don't want
to do anythin' like that again.'

'Only one more,' Carmelita said as she and Sherman
helped Kittredge to his feet. Kittredge looked down at
her. There was a shadow of a smile across her features.

'Maybe I should have insisted on a few more details
before we set off,' he said.

When they moved on, Kittredge could hear the
trickle of running water, and when he put out his hand

he felt a dampness on the rock.

'The water comes from the top of the mesa,' Carmelita said. 'It provides for El Serpiente as it must have provided once for the people who lived up here.'

'Remind me to come back with a team from the Smithsonian,' Kittredge replied.

She looked at him uncomprehendingly.

'Never mind. Let's get on,' he said.

They hadn't gone much further when the path again came to an end, to be replaced by a series of narrow steps cut into the face of the rock.

'Whoever the people were who lived here,' Sherman said, 'they sure worked hard to make themselves secure.'

'I guess that's why Gonsalez chose it,' Kittredge replied.

The steps were uneven and worn away but they were still negotiable.

'Could do with a handrail,' Kittredge said.

Below them the floor of the canyon re-emerged before another bend of the broken stairway took it out of sight again. At one point Sherman slipped but recovered his balance. For the space of a few moments Carmelita looked agitated.

'We must be almost there,' Kittredge said.

As if in reply they came to the final step and emerged on a narrow platform. The path led steeply upwards towards a clump of bushes. Carmelita signalled for them to listen.

'Beyond those bushes the path takes a sharp turn to the right, then we come out at the beginning of the ledge. There are some rocks and some broken houses. The first complete building we come to is the one Gonsalez uses.'

Kittredge was looking about him and straining his ears. 'Can't see or hear anythin',' he said. 'It seems strange to me we ain't been challenged so far.'

'Gonsalez thinks he is secure,' Carmelita told him.

Without waiting for a reply she moved forward. Kittredge and Sherman followed, labouring up the steep slope and into the bushes. In a moment the path levelled and then they saw a glint of light. Carmelita had her knife out and was hacking at some branches which barred the way. In a few seconds she had removed the obstacle and they pushed through the last of the undergrowth to find themselves on the edge of the platform.

It was a dizzying experience. There was a sheer drop to the canyon floor below whilst over their heads the rimrock loomed above the blackness of the cavern which stretched back who knew how far into the cliff. The stone houses of the pueblo, in various stages of disrepair, seemed to cling to the very edge of the precipice although in fact they were set at a reasonable distance back under the shelter of the cavern canopy. The pueblo hung like an eagle's nest and Kittredge had to fight back the same feeling of vertigo he had felt on the rude bridge.

Any further consideration of the situation was ended when Carmelita suddenly moved quickly forward, breaking into a run as she approached the first of the stone houses.

'What's she doin!' Sherman hissed.

For a second Kittredge almost called her name aloud. Then he gasped: 'She's after Gonsalez! Quick, before she ruins everything!'

Both men sprang forward. Carmelita had already passed a couple of buildings and was approaching the next one when suddenly they were halted in their tracks by loud noises coming from the direction of the mountain path they had so laboriously climbed. Instinctively, Kittredge flung himself to the ground.

Sherman stopped dead in his tracks. 'What was that?' he said.

Kittredge couldn't work out what was happening. He looked along the length of the ledge, expecting Gonsalez's men to come rushing out, but there was no movement. Then, from near at hand, he heard something else: a loud creaking and groaning. As he got to his feet it was succeeded by what sounded like some kind of avalanche. He and Sherman had begun to move back along the ledge when a tremendous crash came up from the floor of the canyon. Rushing to the edge, they could see something long and dark which lay across the canyon floor, partly submerged in the stream.

'The bridge!' Sherman snapped. 'They've destroyed the bridge.'

The two men were confused, still not able to work out what was going on. As they tried to make sense of things they heard faint noises from the mountainside, then a few dark, shadowy forms appeared, moving along the canyon floor. The next moment a shot rang

131

out, the reverberations echoing down the canyon. A second shot went singing among the rocks, then a voice called out from the depths below.

'Die, gringo dogs!'

In a flash of insight Kittredge realized what had happened. Gonsalez and some of his men had lured them into a trap and stranded them high on the ledge by toppling the cedar-tree bridge. Hell, no wonder they had seen nothing of Gonsalez's men. Gonsalez must have been aware of their presence all along, and had devised this devilish scheme. As he began to explain his thoughts to Sherman, the figure of Carmelita appeared, coming towards them.

'Gonsalez isn't there,' she said.

As if El Serpiente could hear her words, the voice rose again from the blackness of the canyon floor.

'You too, Carmelita. You thought you could outwit El Serpiente. Now you must share the fate of your friends. Die slowly, *amigos*.' There was the sound of chilling laughter and then silence.

'He has escaped!' Carmelita hissed. 'He is gone.'

'More to the point,' Kittredge said. 'How do we get down from here?'

Sherman was suddenly animated. 'Didn't you say there was a path up to the top of the mesa?' he said to Carmelita.

For a moment she didn't reply. She was still nursing her anger and frustration at having failed to find Gonsalez in his stone refuge.

'Which way is the path?' asked Kittredge.

She looked up at him with flashing eyes.

'We've got to get away from here,' Kittredge insisted. 'Which way do we go?'

Carmelita looked as uncertain as her two companions for some moments. Then she turned towards the far end of the ledge.

'This way,' she breathed.

They followed her along the ledge, past stone houses standing singly or in small groups, over low stone walls and rubble-filled courtyards, till they had almost reached the opposite end of the ledge. Then Carmelita stopped and turned to them.

'The path,' she said. 'It has gone!'

Kittredge ran forward, then halted abruptly. Towards the end of the ledge a portion of rock had fallen away from the wall of the canyon, taking the ledge with it so that it ended in a jagged, gaping descent into nothingness. He stood looking down into the void as the others came up behind him.

'The trail comes down the side of the mountain. Look, you can see part of it high up there.' Carmelita pointed and Kittredge, looking up, could see a thin ribbon of lighter colour beneath the rimrock.

'Is there another way either up or down?' he asked.

Carmelita shook her head. 'There is none that I know of. The trail that is gone would have been almost impassable.'

'Then it looks like we're stranded,' Kittredge said.

Silence descended. Presently Sherman spoke.

'Grattan will come lookin' sooner or later,' he said.

'Yeah,' Kittredge replied. 'But it won't make no difference. It seems there's no way we can get down from here.' He looked up at the sky. There was no sign yet of the approach of dawn.

'There ain't much we can do right now,' he said. 'We might as well try and get some rest.'

Carmelita was still too occupied with her feelings of frustration to seem to care too much about their situation. Without saying anything, she sat down with her back against a wall of one of the buildings.

'One thing we don't have to worry about,' Sherman said. 'There's plenty of water. I guess there should be supplies in some of those buildings, too.'

'Gonsalez too clever to leave supplies,' Carmelita said.

Kittredge had stopped by the remains of one of the fires they had seen earlier. There was still a faint glow left in the embers.

'Gonsalez has been pretty clever,' he remarked. 'But it seems to me that he's decided to abandon the pueblo. Otherwise why would he have come up with this plan?'

'Gonsalez is a snake,' Carmelita said. 'Leaving us here to die slowly would just appeal to him. I wouldn't bet that he hasn't poisoned the water supply.'

'Listen!' Sherman said.

From some little distance they could hear the muffled beat of horses' hoofs.

'Sounds like Gonsalez and his men are ridin' out,' Kittredge said.

The sounds of horses galloping in the night grew louder and then subsided.

'Where do you think he's goin'?' Sherman said.

134

Carmelita laughed bitterly. 'I think he makes for the Spanish Bit,' she said.

Kittredge weighed her remarks and was just about to respond when suddenly the silence of the night was shattered by the sound of gunfire followed by a terrific *BOOM!*

'What the hell was that!' Sherman said.

Carmelita had involuntarily put her hands to her ears. Kittredge glanced up at the sky, thinking that it might be thunder. He thought he could hear some confused sounds but he couldn't be sure what they were. There were a few more sporadic gunshots, then silence. Kittredge looked questioningly at the others, then revelation came.

'Grattan!' he said. 'I reckon that was the Williams gun!'

'Hell, you're right,' Sherman said. 'The old buzzard must have been in the way of the Comancheros headed down the valley, and he loosed off the cannon.'

The three of them lapsed into silence, each thinking the same thing. If Grattan had been caught by the Comancheros, irrespective if whether or not he had fired the gun, it was unlikely that he would have come out of it alive.

CHAPTER SEVEN

The rest of the night dragged by. Kittredge and Sherman dozed fitfully but each time Kittredge opened his eyes it was to see those of Carmelita still wide open. He wouldn't have given much for Gonsalez's chances if she had found him in the stone house. He doubted whether she would have failed twice with her knife.

When the first rays of dawn began to penetrate the canyon they roused themselves and ate some pemmican. Carmelita fetched water in a water jar she found in the courtyard of one of the houses. Ignoring Carmelita's previous statement about the water probably being contaminated, they drank, after which Kittredge examined the receptacle. It was handsomely made and carefully decorated with a geometrical design.

'There are lots like it,' Carmelita said.

They got to their feet and began to examine the village more closely. There were some twenty five dwellings, most of them in an advanced state of disrepair but some still looking much as they might have done when the pueblo was inhabited. Some still showed traces of the pink and yellow shades with which they had originally been tinted. There were signs of their recent occupation by the Comancheros – cigarette ends on the floor, empty bottles – but no food had been left behind. After looking through some of the buildings, they moved back into the cavern which gradually got lower. As their eyes became used to the dark they could see that the roof was darkened by a thick layer of soot.

'They must have used the place for cooking,' Kittredge said.

As if in confirmation they discovered some old clay ovens and some charred bones, then they found something else. At the back there was an opening in the wall which allowed a faint scattering of light to enter the cavern. Kittredge examined it closely.

'Could be some sort of ventilation shaft,' he said.

After striking a match to help relieve the darkness he could see marks on the wall of the cave, which seemed to have been made by some kind of sharp implement. Rock debris still littered the floor together with some larger stones. The surface of the wall was rough and pitted; Kittredge began to push and pull at the gap and immediately he met with success. Some stones loosened and came away. The other two joined him in scrabbling away at the cavern wall. The gap grew larger, then with a crash a big stone dislodged, bringing with it a cascade of debris. Kittredge peered hard inside but could see very little. When he struck another match they could make out a narrow passage winding up into the solid rock.

'Let's get the rest of our gear,' he said.

Carmelita looked at him and he was surprised at the consternation in her expression.

'You are not going to enter the passage?' she said.

'It's a chance we gotta to take,' he replied. 'It might be the only chance we have of gettin' out of here.'

They hurried back to the ledge to collect their belongings. Day had arrived and it took a moment for their eyes to adjust. When they returned to the cave the darkness seemed more palpable. Kittredge struck another match.

'Wish we had a candle,' he said.

He looked into the gap they had uncovered in the cavern wall. It was very narrow. Only one person at a time could enter and even then it would be a squeeze. Carmelita held back and both Kittredge and Sherman could see that she was afraid. Her reaction to the passageway was in stark contrast to her attitude to the dizzy trail up the side of the canyon.

'We'll be right there with you,' Sherman said.

'I'll go first,' Kittredge added. 'Carmelita, you come behind me and Sherman will bring up the rear.'

Kittredge lit another match and stepped into narrow passage. He moved forward, then turned. Carmelita was still hanging back but then, at another word of encouragement from Sherman, she took a step forward. Kittredge could not but help admire her courage. She was clearly in a funk but her resolve still held.

Kittredge moved on, stepping carefully and striking matches at regular intervals to see where he was going.

138

The floor of the passage was remarkably even but the walls were rough and after a time the passage became so narrow that he was forced to turn sideways.

It looked as though they had already reached their limits when the passage unexpectedly widened out again and Kittredge was able to face forwards once more. The passage had been tending upwards and now it began to ascend at a much steeper gradient. Kittredge felt a slight breath of air on his face, then the match he was holding blew out, shrouding them in pitch blackness. But it was only for a moment. Even as he reached for another match he heard a kind of gasp behind him and then the voice of Sherman reassuring Carmelita that everything was OK. He turned back to add his reassurances and when he faced frontward again he saw that the blackness was not absolute. Ahead of him his eyes could distinguish what was undoubtedly a faint patch of light.

His heart thumped. Fumblingly, he struck another match and stepped forward once more. Neither of the other two spoke and he assumed that they had not noticed anything. He quickened his pace a little and moved on. When the match went out he could not see any sign of the light and he thought he must have been mistaken after all. Then the passage took another turn and there it was again ahead of him, faint and indistinct but present. This time the others saw it too.

The passage became steeper and as they approached the patch of light they were treading not stone but earth. They had to bend as the roof came down low at one point, but then it rose again and they had adequate clearance once more. Light was filling the tunnel. Kittredge reached the end. Before him was a wall of earth and a tangle of tree roots through which he could see patches of daylight. He pushed with his shoulder but nothing gave.

'Please,' Carmelita muttered. 'Please find a way out.'

Kittredge pushed as hard as he could but the obstruction seemed immovable.

'Try kickin' at it,' Sherman said.

Kittredge kicked and pushed but the wall of earth did not give. Although the space was cramped Sherman managed to manoeuvre his way past Carmelita and add his weight to the effort.

'Hell,' he muttered. 'There's gotta be a way. We've come this far.'

They both tried again, kicking at the tangle of earth and roots till the sweat began to pour from them. It was a hopeless task. After all their efforts it seemed they were doomed to disappointment. The best they could do would be to make their way back to the cavern. Then suddenly Kittredge had a thought.

'The grenades!' he muttered.

Although he and Sherman had been tempted to leave their equipment behind, they had carried and dragged most of it this far.

'What about the grenades?' Sherman said.

'It's our best chance,' Kittredge replied. 'We're gonna have to blast our way out of here.'

'Are you mad?' Sherman replied. 'More likely if you set one of those things off we'll be buried alive.'

'Take care of Carmelita,' Kittredge replied, 'and

make your way along the passage so you're well back.'

Sherman began to expostulate but then, muttering something beneath his breath, he shuffled backwards, encouraging Carmelita to do the same. Carmelita began to follow him, reacting now like an automaton. Kittredge turned his head and watched till they were out of his sight.

'OK back there?' he shouted.

'Watch what you're doin'!' Sherman's voice replied.

Kittredge took a number of steps backwards. He reached into the bag which lay beside him on the floor and drew out a grenade. He had little experience of the weapon and the ones he had used in the war were of a different type. He could only act on the assumption that the mechanism worked in a similar fashion. That meant that it was important to throw the grenade so that it landed on the plunger.

At a second thought he took out another grenade and placed it next to him. He stepped back just a little further, balanced the missile in his hand and smoothed back the light cloth streamer. On getting out the matches he noticed that there weren't many left. He glanced behind him once more, then struck the match and lit the fuse. Trying to be as careful and accurate as possible, yet putting as much force into his throw as he could muster, he hurled the grenade. Almost in the same motion he grabbed the second, lit the fuse, and threw it after the other. Quickly he turned and started running down the tunnel but he hadn't gone far when there was a dazzling flash of light behind him followed by a tremendous roar and a blast of air. He fell forward on his face as the very walls and floor of the passage seemed to vibrate. Fragments of rock fell on him and the passage was filled with a dense cloud of dust. For a few moments he lay stunned and then, coughing and spluttering, he rose to his knees.

'Everybody all right?' he yelled to the others down the tunnel.

'Yeah! What about you?'

Before he could reply the figures of Sherman and Carmelita appeared through the dust and smoke. Together they hauled Kittredge to his feet. Then, in single file with Sherman leading, they struggled towards the end of the passage. It was hard to see anything but they could sense wind blowing into the tunnel. As they approached they could see a jagged hole where the blockage had been. Tree roots still filled part of it but Sherman was able to force his way through and the next moment they were all out of the passage which had threatened to be their tomb, emerging laughing and slightly hysterical into the clear light of day.

The tunnel had ended beneath the spreading boughs of a stunted piñon tree on the summit of the mesa. When they walked to the nearest edge, they looked down into the canyon from which they had climbed to Gonsalez's aerial roost. They could see nothing of the pueblo because the rim of the mesa overhung the ledge on which the pueblo was built. All around the views were stunning but once they had got used to the idea that they were free, they had other things to consider.

'You say there's a way down from the top of the

mesa?' Kittredge said to Carmelita, who had completely recovered her composure.

'*Sí*, there is a way.'

'Then let's get movin'. We ain't got no time to waste.'

'You thinkin' about Grattan?' Sherman said. 'Boy, those bombs sure saved the day.'

'Yeah. And after we find him, I'm figurin' we'd better get to the Spanish Bit as quick as possible.' He turned back to Carmelita. 'You're pretty sure that's the way Gonsalez would be headed?'

'I am sure,' she replied.

'I'm pretty sure too,' Kittredge said. 'Looks like El Serpiente and his hardcases have decided to move on the Spanish Bit. Once we've checked on Grattan we can pick up our horses.'

'They'd better not have done anythin' to the old fella,' Sherman muttered.

It took longer than Kittredge had imagined for them to descend the mesa. The trail was almost as bad in places as the one they had followed to the pueblo, but eventually they got down. Kittredge was lost and disorientated and the truth of Carmelita's words about the mesa being a strange and mysterious place was borne in upon him. Carmelita, however, showed no hesitation and led the way through a maze of canyons and small hanging meadows till at last they emerged at a place he recognized.

A little further and they saw their horses where they had left them. It had only been the previous evening but it seemed like a long time before. With a feeling of relief they mounted and moved down the trail towards where Grattan had said he would wait with the wagon.

As they got closer a feeling of dread began to grab at Kittredge's guts. If the explosion they had heard during the night had indeed been the Williams gun, what chance would Grattan have had of surviving the encounter with the Comancheros? It was then that they saw the wagon. It lay in smithereens, and tangled up in the wreckage were a number of mangled bodies of men and horses. Kittredge and Sherman slid from their mounts and began to examine the scene of carnage more closely. Carmelita remained on her horse, watching them.

'Can't see no sign of Grattan,' Sherman said.

Kittredge turned over one more body which lay at a little distance from the shattered wagon.

'Nope,' he replied.

Neither of them said a word about what was on their minds: maybe there wasn't too much of Grattan left to find.

'Can't see no trace of those mules either,' Sherman said.

They looked about them. The buzzing of flies was loud in their ears and then another sound rose above it:

The years creep slowly by Lorena,
The snow is on the grass again.

It was the voice of Grattan!

'You old buzzard!' Kittredge shouted. 'Where are you?'

The figure of the oldster appeared round a clump of

bushes. 'I wondered when you'd be back,' he said. 'You sure took your time about it.'

He took a step forward but before he had gone a few paces he stumbled and fell. Kittredge and Sherman both ran towards him while Carmelita quickly dropped from the saddle. The oldster was covered in dirt and grime and his clothes were torn. Across his cheek was a deep gash and there was another cut across his fore-head. As they bent over him his eyes opened and he grinned.

'I never figured the old girl to fire more'n one shot anyway,' he said. 'Lucky she managed that.'

Later, as they sat round a fire, Grattan told them what had happened. Carmelita had patched him up and he was fine except for a bad headache. He had retired for the night, taking some of the remaining grenades with him, when he heard the sound of the approaching Comancheros. There were too many of them and he had fled for cover where he had left the mules.

Most of the Comancheros had swept past without even seeing the wagon but a few had stopped to inves-tigate. Some of them were drunk already before they began helping themselves to Grattan's supplies of liquor. They had begun to fight and argue among themselves. They were obviously puzzled about the gun and things must have gone on from there.

Grattan had approached rather too close, when the gun exploded. He had been hit by flying metal. There wasn't much left of the Comancheros. He had crawled back into cover and remembered nothing more till he woke up and heard the voice of Kittredge yelling his name.

'You were singin',' Kittredge said.

'Yeah? I kinda remember dreamin' . . .' His voice tailed off. Then, after some moments: 'What about you fellas?' he said, including Carmelita in the circle.

Quickly they gave an account of what had happened.

'How many of those grenades we got left?' Grattan asked when they had finished.

'Why do you want to know?' Sherman replied.

The oldster grinned again. ' 'Cos I figure we ain't done with 'em yet,' he said. 'Figure they might come in useful when we get to the Spanish Bit.'

The next morning before dawn they saddled up, and rode out of the mesa, Grattan taking one of the loose uninjured Comanchero horses.

Crudace had made himself comfortable at the Spanish Bit. More important, he had prepared his defences and his men were ready for the fight which Crudace sensed was coming. He reckoned it was only a question of time before Gonsalez made his play and he was ready for whatever El Serpiente might throw at him. The Spanish Bit was on a war footing.

The way he figured it, Gonsalez would not be expecting any resistance when he arrived at the Spanish Bit. After all, he was well known there and there would be no reason for him to expect any trouble. Much less would there be any reason for him to suspect that the place had been strengthened by the arrival of Crudace and his heavies from the Scissors.

146

Crudace's plan was simple: he would let Gonsalez ride into the yard of the Spanish Bit and cut him down there. He had men placed in all the strategic positions, hidden from sight and well briefed. Now he only had to wait.

He was sitting on the veranda with his rifle on his knees when a rider galloped into the yard to tell him that Gonsalez had been sighted.

'Good. Put your horse in the stable and then take up your position.'

Crudace stepped out into the yard and waved his arms as the signal that Gonsalez was on his way. Then he went inside the ranch house to take up his own position by an upstairs window. He peered through the curtains, checking that his men were concealed. He could see nothing, which meant it was even more unlikely that Gonsalez would detect anything.

'That no-good rattlesnake's time has come,' he said to the watcher by the other window. It was Crombie, his foreman.

Crombie chuckled. 'This is gonna be fun,' he said.

They waited while the only sound to disturb the silence was the ticking of a clock. Crudace looked around once more. The men were well hidden. Then he heard the sound of approaching hoofbeats. Looking beyond an outbuilding, he saw a growing cloud of dust which could only mean Gonsalez was at hand. He glanced across to the man at the opposite window and licked his lips. Crudace was to fire the first shot which would be the signal for the others to open fire.

The rhythm of approaching hoofs grew louder and

through the dust Crudace could see the leading figures. As he had anticipated, Gonsalez was showing no sign of apprehension or awareness of danger. If anything, he was being cockier than ever. It would have been sensible for him to have come under the guise of bringing in a herd of cattle but he obviously felt no need of subterfuge.

The bunch of riders came on, Gonsalez at their head. Soon they would be in the yard and when they started to dismount Crudace would fire that first shot, the one which would put Gonsalez out of action. Already Crudace's finger was caressing the trigger of his rifle when the riders suddenly drew to a halt.

'What the hell's goin' on?' Crudace hissed.

'Reckon they figure somethin's not right. Maybe the place is too quiet.'

Crudace cursed beneath his breath. Had he been too efficient? Maybe he should have allowed some sign of activity taking place in order to avoid any suspicions on the part of El Serpiente. Presumably he hadn't earned that sobriquet for nothing. He craned his neck to see what was happening. Gonsalez was saying something to another man who had ridden up alongside him. The man responded by rising in his stirrups and looking about. The conversation resumed and then, to Crudace's relief, Gonsalez gave a signal and the band of Comancheros started forward again. Crudace tried counting them but gave up. There were a lot of them.

Crudace became aware that sweat had broken out on his brow and was running down his neck. He felt nervous. His mouth was dry and he licked his lips again.

148

He glanced at the man at the other window but Crombie was intent on observing what was happening outside. A sickly feeling grew in Crudace's stomach. Without him being aware of it, his finger tightened on the trigger of his rifle and he almost fell back with the ricochet as the weapon barked and the bullet flew harmlessly into the air.

'What are you doin'?' Crombie said. 'They ain't reached the yard yet.'

The next moment the place was rent apart by a furious outburst of gunfire emanating from the ranch buildings. Some of the Comancheros went down while others tried to turn their horses in the direction from which they had come. Some leaped from the saddle to find what shelter they could. It didn't take them long to realize what was happening and they began returning fire with remarkable speed and accuracy. Bullets crashed through the open windows of the ranch house and thudded into the walls. Crudace felt a sharp pang of pain; blood was flowing down his cheek.

'I've been hit!' he yelled. 'Help me, I've been hit!'

Crombie looked across at him. 'It's nothin',' he yelled back. 'You've caught a splinter of wood from the window frame. Keep down and out of sight!'

In response Crudace whimpered and, throwing his rifle aside, began to crawl across the floor. Crombie looked at him disbelievingly but his attention was quickly occupied in returning fire as a bullet whined into the room and crashed into the opposite wall. The next moment Crudace had gone, disappearing on his hands and knees through the open door. Crombie picked up a second rifle and resumed firing.

The yard below was littered with bodies and the amount of fire coming from the Comancheros had diminished. Rifle fire was still raining down from the roof of the barns and stables where most of the Spanish Bit men were hidden and Crombie assumed that most of them were still unhurt, despite Crudace's botched signal. He looked around for Crudace but he was gone.

'Doggone yellow coyote!' he muttered.

Firing was now very sporadic and Crombie took the opportunity to leave his post and make for the door. Where was Crudace? He looked along the corridor but there was no sign of him. He looked down the stairwell. Nothing. He had a glimpse of one of the men down there reloading his rifle. Before he had time to consider the matter further, there came a fresh burst of gunfire and he crawled back inside the room.

The gunfire was succeeded by comparative calm, then he heard mingled noises coming from somewhere beyond his range of vision. He caught the sound of hoofs and had a glimpse of a couple of horsemen riding hard in the direction of the corrals. There came a burst of cheering from the rooftops, then someone shouted:

'They've had enough! They're runnin'!'

There was a fresh burst of cheering and some further desultory shots; various figures began to emerge from their places of concealment and gather in the yard. Forgetting Crudace for a moment, Crombie gave a whoop and ran down the stairs to join them. There was no doubt that they had won the day. Comanchero corpses lay all about and those still surviving had made a run for it. Somebody suggested riding after them but no one took up the suggestion. Instead they began to look about for Gonsalez. By the time they had searched the place and piled up the bodies in one of the barns, it was clear that Gonsalez must have escaped. It didn't matter to the victors. As far as they were concerned, Gonsalez had been taught a lesson he wouldn't forget. There would be no more to fear from him. But where was Crudace?

Even as they were asking the question, that gentleman was riding hard in the general direction of what he thought would lead him eventually back to the town of Arrowhead and the Scissors ranch. In fact, such was his terror and confusion, he was heading in precisely the opposite direction. He had escaped through a back window of the ranch and captured a stray horse. Now his one intent was to get away from the Spanish Bit and the scene of conflict as quickly as possible.

The sounds of battle dwindled to his rear. He kept going till his horse was covered in sweat and flagging badly, then at last he drew to a halt. He was still quaking and the prospect of the long ride ahead of him filled him with dread. He put his hand up to his face where blood was trickling from the cuts he had received from the shards of wood.

Another possibility struck him. He could ride back to the Spanish Bit. Thinking about it, he burst into a ragged laugh. Of course, it was the obvious thing to do. It was his ranch, after all, and they were his men. It might be a bit awkward facing them, but he could make up some kind of story. Yes, it was the only realistic course of action.

He was just about to turn his horse when it occurred to him that there was no guarantee the Comancheros had been beaten. What if they had won the day and the Spanish Bit was now in Gonsalez's hands? Swearing out loud, he cursed his own foolishness in having fired his rifle too soon and given the game away. If he had waited till Gonsalez and his gang of Comancheros were gathered in the yard, as had been the intention, he could have been sure of killing them all.

Still puzzling about it, he looked up and saw a little plume of dust on the landscape, something he had not noticed before. Preoccupied with his thoughts, he watched it as it grew steadily larger, and even when it became clear that it was the dust thrown up by a rider he did not at first register any particular emotion. Through the shimmering heat haze the form of the rider began to emerge and for the first time Crudace's numbed senses registered a warning. The figure came closer and Crudace could begin to distinguish some of its features. With something like a cold hand of ice gripping his heart he recognized Gonsalez. Even then he did nothing. He was mesmerized like a prairie dog in the gaze of a rattlesnake. Gonsalez galloped the last few remaining yards and then pulled up hard so that his horse reared in front of Crudace.

'So, you try to kill El Serpiente,' he said. 'You thought to catch El Serpiente in a trap. Well, my friend, as you can see, I have escaped your trap.'

He turned in the saddle and threw out his arm in a

152

sweeping gesture. Far off, another cloud stained the horizon like smoke. 'Many of my men die but others escape. See, they follow El Serpiente.'

Crudace's eyes glanced at the dust cloud which was formed by those of Gonsalez's men who had managed to ride away from the Spanish Bit. Before he realized what was happening he felt a sharp crack and the next moment his arms were pinioned to his sides by Gonsalez's lariat.

'Prepare to die, gringo pig,' Gonsalez shouted.

He gave a tug and Crudace was lifted from his saddle, falling with a heavy crash to the ground. He let out a yell of pain but it was drowned in the sound of Gonsalez's laughter and the clatter of his horse's hoofs as he dug his spurs into the animal's flanks. It began to move, soon breaking into a trot as it dragged the hapless land agent behind it. The ground was rough and stony. In a matter of moments Crudace's face was a hideous mess of blood and mangled flesh as his tormented, terrified screams faded away into the silent desert air. His bones cracked and snapped but Gonsalez kept on riding. When he stopped to await the arrival of his men there wasn't much about Crudace that was still recognizable.

Four other people watched as the cloud of dust Gonsalez had pointed out to Crudace travelled across the desert. They were Kittredge, Sherman, Grattan and Carmelita. Kittredge took his field glasses from their case and put them to his eyes.

'Comancheros,' he said. 'Headed this way.'

'Let me take a look,' Carmelita responded. She

looked closely at the advancing horsemen. 'Some of Gonsalez's men,' she said. 'They must be riding back to the mesa.'

They pondered the situation for a moment.

'My guess is, they've hit trouble at the Spanish Bit and are retreating to their hideout,' Sherman said.

Grattan spat into the sand. 'We still got some of those grenades left,' he said.

Kittredge gave him a quizzical look.

'They worked in the tunnel,' Grattan added.

Carmelita pointed to some rocks. 'If we wait there, Gonsalez's men will ride close by. It is the ideal spot.'

'The ideal spot to get ourselves killed,' Kittredge said.

'If the – what you say – grenades – don't work, we have the rocks for cover. We'd have a better chance there anyway.'

They could all see the sense of her comments.

'Come on,' Kittredge said. 'Let's do as Carmelita says.'

They rode into the cover of the rocks and dismounted. Leaving their horses well out of sight, they took up a position among the rocks from which they had a good view of the approaching horsemen. The remaining grenades were placed near by. Kittredge continued to observe the riders through his field glasses.

'Let me take another look,' Carmelita said. She took some time examining the riders before handing the glasses back.

'Gonsalez is among them,' she said. 'He is riding at the back.'

Kittredge took another look through the glasses, curious to know what Gonsalez looked like.

'There's only ten of 'em altogether,' he remarked. 'Didn't you say he had many followers?'

'They must have been killed,' Carmelita said.

'I think Sherman's got it right,' Grattan interposed. 'I reckon they bit off more than they could chew by attackin' the Spanish Bit.'

Kittredge agreed. He was struck for a moment by the irony of the fact that it seemed one of his enemies had been instrumental in destroying the other. He couldn't know till they discovered Crudace's mangled corpse just how ironic the situation was. The riders were getting close.

'What do you think?' Kittredge said, addressing the rest in general.

Sherman, ignoring the field glasses, had been peering intently at the Comancheros.

'They look like a beaten bunch to me,' he said.

Grattan spat again. 'You won't get no more trouble from Gonsalez,' he said. 'He's lost most of his men, he's lost his hideout and he's lost his reputation. I figure he's gonna ride on clear over the border.'

'You forget, he has probably left some of his men behind to look after the cattle,' Carmelita said.

'Maybe a few. From what we saw, I'd say mighty few. There's no need. Those cow critters got everythin' they want up there and they ain't likely to bust loose.'

'I figure those cows are gonna be just fine till we round 'em up and take 'em back where they belong,' Kittredge said.

'So, what are you suggestin'? That we don't do anythin', just let Gonsalez go?'

Kittredge glanced at Sherman and then at Grattan. 'I'm gettin' kinda tired of all this killin',' he said. 'Besides, we might have the advantage with those grenades, but who's to say they won't turn out to be damp squibs?'

'Or blow up in our hands,' Sherman replied. He looked at Grattan but, remembering what had happened with the Williams gun, the oldster remained silent.

'We'll let 'em go,' Kittredge said.

The Comancheros were now only a short distance away and their passage would take them underneath where they were hiding among the rocks.

'Lie still,' Kittredge said.

The first of the riders came abreast of them and then the main body, raising clouds of dust which blew into the faces of the watchers above them. They had almost passed and Kittredge was about to relax when suddenly he became conscious of a movement to his right. Before he had any time to react Carmelita had flung herself from the rock to land upon Gonsalez's horse as it brought up the rear of the group. Kittredge saw a flash of light and then the horse went over, throwing Gonsalez and Carmelita to the ground. She was the first to her feet and Kittredge watched in horror as Carmelita buried her knife to the hilt in Gonsalez's back.

For a moment he lay there before struggling to his knees, then falling forward, the hilt of the knife pro-

156

truding from between his shoulder blades. Carmelita walked forward and muttered something which Kittredge could not catch before pushing at the body with her foot so that it rolled to its side.

The thing had happened in an instant and none of the Comancheros appeared for the moment to have noticed anything. The whole thing seemed unreal, then suddenly one of the Comancheros shouted and they drew to a halt. The next moment there was a burst of gunfire and bullets went ricocheting around the rocks. Kittredge seized his rifle and began to return fire when there was a loud roar and the desert exploded into flame and smoke.

When his senses had recovered Kittredge realized that Grattan had thrown one of the grenades. His aim hadn't been very good because, as far as Kittredge could see, only one of the Comancheros had gone down. The horses were screaming in fear and the Comancheros were having difficulties controlling them as they reared and ploughed, whinnying in terror. As Kittredge and Sherman commenced to fire again, the Comancheros appeared to have had enough. Almost with one accord they began to swing their horses away from the rocks and gallop in disarray from the scene. Kittredge watched their retreating forms for a few moments through the shimmering desert air, then held up his hand as a signal to stop shooting.

'What the hell happened?' Sherman shouted. He had not seen Carmelita's plunge from the rock.

Kittredge jumped to his feet. 'Keep me covered,' he shouted, just in case the Comanchero who had been affected by the explosion was still active. In an instant he had vaulted over the rocks to where the body of Gonsalez lay bleeding in the sand. He could not see what had become of Carmelita but the next moment he detected her legs protruding from a rock. He ran to her side and found her lying stunned and bruised but otherwise unhurt.

'That was stupid!' he began. 'You could have got us all killed.'

She looked up at him. 'I kill Gonsalez,' she said. 'El Serpiente bad man. Now he no more.'

Kittredge helped her to her feet just as the figure of Sherman appeared.

'Gonsalez is dead,' he confirmed. 'And so is the other one.'

To the surprise of both men, Carmelita turned to Sherman and put her head on his chest. Sherman looked in some consternation at Kittredge.

'I'm gonna have a word with Grattan,' Kittredge said.

Late that night Kittredge and Sherman were sitting by the campfire. Carmelita had turned in for the night. Out in the surrounding darkness they could see the light of Grattan's cheroot which he had found somewhere as he checked on the horses and mules.

'Well,' Sherman said. 'Seems like we dealt with those Comancheros.'

'I can't help feelin' some pity for Crudace,' Kittredge said. 'No matter how bad he was, he came to an awful end.'

'Sure did,' Sherman replied. 'You're certain Gonsalez was responsible?'

'Who else could it have been?' Kittredge replied.

They lapsed into silence, neither liking to dwell on what they had found late that afternoon. They had buried Crudace where he lay.

After a time they heard shuffling footsteps and Grattan rejoined them.

'Well, old fella,' Kittredge said. 'What next for you?'

Grattan blew a cloud of smoke through his nostrils.

'Don't rightly know,' he replied. 'Carry on tradin', I guess.'

'You ain't got no wagon and no stock any more.'

'Yeah, you got a point there.'

Sherman laughed. 'While you're thinkin' it over,' he said, 'I figure Waggoner could work out somethin' for you to do about the Rafter W. Especially with your engineerin' skills an' all.'

Kittredge glanced at the sleeping form of Carmelita.

'What do we do with her?' he asked.

Sherman gave them both a sheepish look.

'Oh, I see,' said Kittredge. 'Man, I wish you the best of luck. Remember how she dealt with Gonsalez.'

'Not to mention yourself, Sherman,' Grattan intervened.

'She's kinda wild,' Sherman said. 'I'll give you that. Reckon I'll take my chances.'

'Once we get back to the Rafter W we'll call on the marshal and get him to come down here with a few of the boys from the ranch. That way we can straighten out matters with the Spanish Bit.'

'Yeah, and drive those cattle that rightly belong to us back to the home range again.'

159

'It'll be interestin' to go back to that mesa,' Kittredge said.

They poured what was left of the coffee brewing on the flames into their cups.

'We've talked about me and Grattan,' Sherman said. 'What you figurin' to do, Kittredge?'

Kittredge smacked his lips and looked into the fire. 'Reckon I could still link up with that trail drive to Abilene,' he said.

'Yeah, reckon you could. On the other hand, you could stay with the Rafter W.'

Kittredge seemed to consider it for a few moments. 'There's work to be done,' he replied.

Sherman grinned. 'Sure is. A lot of work.'

'Maybe startin' with a certain young lady name of Miss Trashy?' Grattan intervened. Kittredge looked at the oldster.

'Don't figure you'll be needin' any of those grenades,' Grattan said. 'Nor the big gun neither, for that matter. Nope sirree. I reckon you're gonna have plenty explosive material without any help from me.'